Jennifer Greene

Arizona Heat

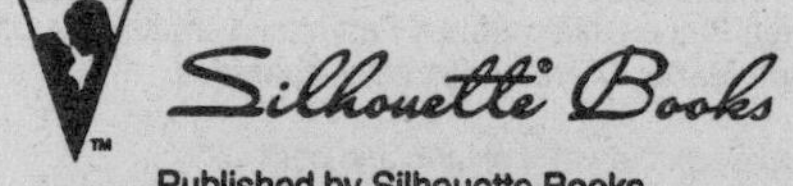

Published by Silhouette Books
America's Publisher of Contemporary Romance

ISBN 0-373-36006-1

ARIZONA HEAT

This edition published by arrangement with Harlequin Books S.A.

Visit Silhouette Books at www.eHarlequin.com

Printed in U.S.A.

JENNIFER GREENE

lives near Lake Michigan with her husband and two children. Before writing full-time, she worked as a teacher and a personnel manager. Michigan State University honored her as an "outstanding woman graduate" for her work with women on campus.

Ms. Greene has written more than fifty category romances, for which she has won numerous awards, including two RITA® Awards from the Romance Writers of America in the Best Short Contemporary Books category, and a Career Achievement Award from *Romantic Times BOOKclub.*

One

Lord, it was hot. Baking hot, choking hot, underwear-sticking hot. Kansas McClellan slapped at the insect buzzing around her neck with a scowl.

She'd been in southern Arizona all of twenty-four hours. Long enough to hate it. Sweat was drooling behind her knees; her calf muscles were screaming from the long hike; and redheads with delicate skin were simply not built to tolerate a climate with all this confounded, relentless *sun.*

Minnesota in May was a splendiferously superb place to live. Daffodils and lilacs in bloom.

Lots of cool, clear lakes. Lots of dark, shady woods.

Kansas slapped another bug, musing that she'd sell her soul—without a qualm—for an ounce of shade right now. She was probably going to end up with heat stroke before this little adventure was over. For sure, she was going to end up with freckles. Naturally this impromptu trip had come up too fast for her to think about details like packing sunscreen. Her throat was parched. Her sandals hurt. Her daffodil yellow shorts and scoop-neck T-shirt were as close to naked as she could get without risking arrest. The outfit still felt hotter than a glued-on suit of armor. Briefly she indulged in a wanton, enticing fantasy about swimming stark naked in a cool mountain lake.

The fantasy was almost better than sex. Regretfully it didn't last any longer than most men—but ahead, as she turned a corner, she found something more exciting than either. Just ahead was shade, real shade, *serious* shade...and the glimpse of a low-roofed building.

When she'd parked her rental car near the sign for the Mile Hi Ramsey Canyon Preserve, she had no idea it would be such a hike to the actual place—or that the landscape could conceivably change this fast. Suddenly there were trees instead of bleak, bald desert. Suddenly there was *green.* Suddenly—she saw the closed door to the building—there was a prayer of civilized air-conditioning.

Ignoring the heat, she aimed for the door at a breakneck sprint. Seconds later, she was inside the preserve office and basking in the immediate cool.

With a single glance, she could see she fit in here as well as a stripper on Wall Street. The dozen people milling around were all appropriately decked out in L.L. Bean and Patagonia labels. Her overbright shorts outfit had come from Marianne's—on sale. Half the L-shaped room was an active bookstore, stocked with extensive references and tomes on the wildlife and geology of the area. Personally, Kansas favored romances.

Being a fish out of water rarely bothered her. At twenty-nine, she'd been a misfit so long that the title fit as comfortably as a pair of well-worn jeans. There were just a few times when she wished she had the gift for fitting in—like now. If she were ever going to find her younger brother in this dadblasted desert country, Kansas needed help.

Years ago, she'd have swallowed a bullet before admitting needing help for anything. As a kid, she'd been tough. She'd been stubborn.

She'd also been proud, to the point of stupidity—a lesson she'd learned the hard way and didn't intend to repeat.

Impatiently she waited her turn to speak with the woman behind the front desk. Apparently only small groups were allowed in the Preserve at a time, and a cluster of college-age kids stood ahead of her, pleading their case to the head honcho lady. From listening to their conversation, Kansas gathered that the canyon was the site of an annual hummingbird migration, that said-migration was spectacular, and that this spring was a one-of-a-kind viewing experience for hummingbird enthusiasts.

She blew a limp, carrot-top curl out of her eyes. She had no quarrel with the hummingbird lovers. She just had another agenda, and the day was wasting—the hour was already past three.

Finally the kids turned around and jostled past her. Kansas stepped up and cleared her throat, suddenly unsure how to phrase her question. The round-faced young woman took one glance at her looks and attire, and immediately assumed why she was here.

"You're lost, right?" The lady's tone was amused, but not unkind.

"No. At least, not exactly. I know this is going

to sound a little strange, but I'm looking for a man—''

''Aren't we all,'' the woman murmured.

Kansas chuckled, and relaxed. ''Actually, right now, I'm trying to locate a specific man—a vet. A Dr. Moore. Paxton Moore. I can't imagine that you'd automatically know every single person who happens to be in the Preserve, but I've been calling his office since early this morning, and all I keep getting is an answering machine message that he's here—''

''The doc? Sure, he's here. No problem.''

The way the woman's face lit up, Kansas gathered that nothing about the ''doc'' was ever a potential problem. As quick as a blink, she was given directions and aimed back outside toward the main trail. Another hike. And uphill yet. Swell.

Another hundred and fifty miles later, she found the man. At least, he appeared to be her quarry, since he was hunched over an extremely fat raccoon with an injured paw. The raccoon was wide-awake. And noticeably not a happy camper. The critter wasn't winning the wrestling match, but it definitely expressed some violently negative opinions about the white bandage being wrapped around its right paw.

Kansas faked a delicate cough. ''Excuse me. Are you Dr. Moore?''

No glance in her direction, no startled surprise at being interrupted. Just a ''Yup. Be with you in a second.''

She was happy to wait, partly because it gave her a chance to catch her breath and quit huffing and puffing, and partly because she wanted—needed—a chance to study him.

Maybe he was a vet, but somehow she couldn't see Dr. Moore catering to the poodle trade.

She guessed his age in the early thirties, and there had to be some Native American genes in his bloodline somewhere. His hair was Apache black, worn thick and straight and long enough to rubber-band into a ponytail. His skin was bronzed darker than gold, with high cheekbones carved into a long, strong, angular face.

Given a little face paint and a pony, and she could easily picture him licking Custer a few years back. Maybe single-handed. He wasn't carrying an ounce of spare weight, but his shoulders and chest tested the seams of a worn navy T-shirt, and his old jeans explicitly defined long muscled thighs. Cords of veins flexed in his upper arms. There was no sweat on him, even though it was four hundred degrees, and the big hands working on the raccoon were competent and patient. It didn't seem to bother him—if he noticed at all—that the critter was raising holy hell.

He was built for a fight, Kansas mused, but he was also unbelievably gentle with the wounded animal. Both qualities reassured her. For her brother's sake, she would have sought out Godzilla if she had to—but dealing with a Godzilla-type would have been exhausting if not downright unproductive. She needed a man who could help her. Assuming she could talk him into it.

Eventually he finished the bandaging chore and let the raccoon free. Still sitting on his haunches, he watched how the critter handled its newfound mobility for several more minutes before glancing up. "You're looking for me?"

"Yes. If you're Dr. Paxton Moore—"

"Pax." He immediately corrected her, and pushed off from his knees to stand.

Her pulse suddenly bucked like a nervous colt. Until that instant, the only thought that crossed her mind was about how this man might relate to her brother. It never occurred to her that she might have a personal reaction to him.

When he stood, though, he loomed over her. Maybe, if she were on tiptoe, the crest of her head might reach his chin. That long, angular face had character lines on his brow, a cleft in his cheek and eyes that made her think of skinny-dipping in a deep, dark lake at midnight—they were that black. That sexy. Even for a woman who was sick to death of men—and Kansas had judiciously avoided all species with a y chromosome for a long, peaceful year now—she didn't figure any female on the planet could fail to perk up around this one. For a look at *those* eyes, a woman might even be tempted to wake up from a coma.

"Pax," she agreed, and stuck out her hand. "My name is Kansas McClellan. And every which way I've turned since arriving in Sierra Vista, your name keeps cropping up as the only person who can help me."

"Sounds doubtful. Somebody's either giving me compliments or insults that I probably don't deserve." His smile was slow, his gaze shrewd and assessing as he clasped her hand for a millisecond and let it go. "What's the problem? Sick animal?"

"No. A missing brother." She saw the swift judgment mirrored in his eyes. It took no special perception to guess what he thought. She knew the image she projected—a bitsy, frail looking redhead, likely a sissy and definitely a wimp. Most men looked at her and immediately assumed she was a lightweight who needed protecting. Correcting that misconception required so much patience, time and aggravation that Kansas had finally thrown in the towel. It had been a lot easier on her heart to just give up men altogether.

Just then, though, Kansas had no time for pride. The irony prickled her sense of humor—for the first time in her life, she wanted a man to judge her solely by her appearance. If Pax saw her as frail, fragile and delicate, he might be more inclined to help her, and pulling off a "wimp" image took no acting. She was wilting miserably in the heat, and she noticed his gaze zipped immediately above her neck, earning him major brownie points as a gentleman. God knew, she had no figure to fret over, but her shorts and top were damply clinging and sticking in embarrassing places.

She forged ahead to explain. "My brother's name is Case. Case Walker. We don't have the same last name—different dads—but we were always as close as glue. I'm scared. Which is why I flew down here from home. Home is Minnesota. Anyway, Case is nineteen, doesn't look like me, blue eyes, brown hair, a good looker and a little hefty—around 200 pounds—"

"I know him." Pax interrupted her.

Some of the tension sagged out of her shoulders. ''Good. I thought you did, because he'd mentioned your name in some of his letters. And that's what other people told me, too—that you were kind to Case and helped him out when he first moved down here—''

''Why are you scared?''

''Because I haven't heard from him in several weeks now. Neither has anyone in the family. Actually no one likely would have, but me. Case hasn't exactly been winning prizes for maturity and responsibility with the family for the past couple of years. He's having a little trouble finding his way, but he's basically wonderful, a heart as big as the sky—''

Possibly Pax noticed her teensy tendency to ramble, because he interrupted again. ''He was running away when he came here.''

''He's just not quite ready to settle down,'' Kansas instantly defended him.

''Whatever. If he disappeared from sight, could be he just got itchy feet again. Do you have some specific reason to worry?''

All these precise questions. Kansas pushed a hand through her snarled mass of curls. Precise questions weren't exactly her forte. ''He always wrote me, once a week. Occasionally we talked on the phone, too, but he was as regular as a clock with those letters. He just seemed more comfortable spilling out what was on his mind in written form. And I haven't had a letter now in three weeks.''

Pax nodded. ''Still not necessarily reason to worry. He could have gone off with some friends, taken a vacation.''

''He's in trouble,'' Kansas said.

''You know that for sure?''

''Yes.''

''How do you know that?''

''Because I love him,'' she said irritably, and smacked at a bug hovering around her chest. She smacked so hard her chest stung, but Dr. Moore was starting to rattle her. Clearly he was one of those rational men who thought things through logically. How were they ever going to communicate? ''I know my brother better than anyone on earth. Maybe it sounds crazy, but I've always had an intuition about when Case was in trouble. I don't know if he's hurt. I just know that something is wrong, really wrong, and somehow I have to get someone to believe me—''

''Now just take it easy,'' Pax said, more slowly, more gently. His gaze drifted over her face again. ''I never said that I didn't believe you. I was just trying to get some straight answers. And I still don't know what you want from me.''

''I was hoping you knew where Case is. Or that you could help me find him.''

''I don't know where he is. And yeah, I noticed he wasn't around for the past few weeks. But as you said, your brother doesn't exactly ace the course in dependability—or predictability.''

''This is different,'' she said firmly.

''Pretty clear that you believe it is.''

''I only arrived in town last night. Without knowing anything about the area or his friends, the best I could think of to do was knock on his neighbors' doors. But no one knows anything. No one's seen him. The only lead I ever picked up from his letters was you. And his neighbors said you'd know if anyone would, and also that you did some tracking—like finding people, campers or whatever, if they got lost in the canyons around here...*damn,* how can anyone *think* in this blasted heat!''

Well, who would have guessed that an exasperated complaint would finally coax a smile from him? And not that stingy ghost of a smile like before, Kansas noted, but a full-fledged charmer of a grin. So...he wasn't stone. His expression revealed so little of what he was thinking that she'd started to worry that he was one of those emotionally constipated types—no one she could conceivably relate to.

"I'm getting the feeling you're not too fond of our desert country." Without asking, he unhooked the canvas-wrapped canteen from his belt loop and handed it to her.

"I'll never complain about another Minnesota blizzard again." Gratefully she took the canteen, twisted the cap and mainlined several gulps thirstily. The water was warm, but she didn't care. It was wet. Throat-drenching, sweet, soft, wet. Nectar couldn't taste any better. "Thanks. You saved my life."

"I think you'd probably have survived a few minutes more," he said wryly. When she returned it, he recapped the canteen and clipped it back to his belt. "You might want to remember, though, if you're traveling much around here, it's wise to carry some water on you."

"If it were a vacation choice, I'd be in Alaska. The last time I remember being this miserable, I was laid up with the flu. This is supposed to be a healthy climate, huh? How many times have I read that you don't feel the heat because it's dry heat? What a total lie. Even my fingernails feel roasted from the inside out."

Damned if she didn't win another irresistibly

male grin. ''If you just got here, you're bound to have a little trouble adjusting to the climate.''

She shook her head. ''Adjusting is not an option. Obviously you've never been a redhead or you'd understand—the sun hates me. It was never anything I had a vote about. I don't suppose there's a way to air-condition the outdoors?''

''I don't believe so,'' he said dryly.

''Well, then, it's hopeless. Write me off as a city sissy, but I just don't think southern Arizona and I were ever meant to get along.'' Kansas mentally shook her head when he let out a deep, throaty chuckle. She'd never planned on running on so long, but darned if it wasn't working. All she'd had to do was honestly admit how miserable she was and make a little fun of herself. The starch left his shoulders; the formal reserve disappeared from his expression. If humor and honesty softened him up, she mused, they might just conceivably get along. She'd never have been able to find common ground with anyone who didn't have a sense of humor.

''You don't have to be here long,'' he consoled her.

''You've got that right. I'll only be here long enough to find my brother. But I can't...'' She lost the thought, diverted by the sudden flash and sparkle of something moving in the corner of her vision. Although ornithology had never been her hobby, she still knew enough to recognize a hummingbird. She'd just never seen one like this.

All kinds of trees and scraggly bushes bordered the trail, but unlike the emeralds and deep greens of woods in Minnesota, everything here was a sun-bleached and dusty dull green—which was probably why the bird riveted her attention. It was so startlingly bright and gaudy. Although it couldn't be bigger than the cup of her hand, the dizzy bird dove like a whirling dervish, swooping and spinning as if the whole sky were its playground. Its head and beak were dark, but the hummingbird's neck appeared to be wearing a collar of iridescent spangles in a glittering scarlet red that caught and reflected the sun.

Pax turned his head to find what she was looking at. "It's Anna's," he said.

"You mean the bird belongs to someone named Anna?"

"No, I mean that's the name of the species. Anna's Hummingbird. Calypte Anna. More than a dozen different species migrate to the canyon around this time of year, peaking around the month of May. They've got a name for the hummingbirds around here—jewels of the sky."

''That's exactly how that one looks, as if it were covered in jewels.'' She shielded her eyes with a cupped hand. ''Do they all fly like that? Like drunk kamikaze pilots?''

He chuckled. ''I strongly suspect there's a girl somewhere in the trees that he's trying to impress.''

''Ah. Hormones. The great equalizer in life. The one thing guaranteed to make fools out of every species in the kingdom, isn't it?'' She couldn't take her eyes off the beauty. ''I'm afraid the daredevil's gonna crash land and kill himself.''

''If any other bird tried that, he probably would.'' Pax hunkered down to gather his first aid and vet supplies. Instead of a traditional doctor's black bag, he carried a hiker's backpack. ''Critters are my business, but there's no explaining anything hummingbirds do. They break every natural law in the books.''

''No kidding? Like what?''

''Well...for one thing, the aerodynamic experts claim that the hummer's wing and body structure should make it impossible to fly—but they're outstanding flyers. They're also the squirts of the bird kingdom, the tiniest in body size yet with the biggest wing span—breaking another universal physics law about weight and body proportion. And any biologist can tell you they're not anatomically built to hover, much less hover over flowers for long periods of time—yet they're excellent at that, too. Hummingbirds may look tiny and fragile, but they have a long history of doing the impossible. They just do it *their* way, and to hell with everybody else's rules."

Kansas didn't look away until the hummingbird had disappeared from sight. Abruptly she discovered that Pax was standing beside her. He had packed up the supplies he'd used on the raccoon, and the knapsack was strapped to his back, as if he were ready to leave. But not at that exact instant. At that exact instant, his eyes were focused on her face with a look of such concentrated speculation that—if it hadn't been broiling hot—she might have shivered.

"What?" she asked him.

"Nothing. It just crossed my mind how often appearances are misleading. Something tells me you're not real fond of doing anything by anyone else's rule book, either."

Her cinnamon eyebrows feathered up. "Hoboy, you couldn't be more wrong. I'm not only big on rules, but what you see is what you get. I thought you already figured it out—I'm a city wimp. Gutless. Weak. Helpless anywhere away from my air-conditioning."

"Yeah?"

"Oh, yeah. Which was how I was hoping to convince you that I seriously, honestly need help finding my brother. I just have no possible way to cope alone."

Pax checked in at the preserve office, then gave Kansas a lift in his dusty Explorer to the inconceivably long distance she'd parked her rental car.

"Thanks," she said fervently. When she hopped out, though, she didn't immediately leave, but crossed her arms in the open truck window on the passenger side. "Seven o'clock tonight, right? And you know where my brother's place is?"

The lady, Pax thought, was relentless. She could wear down a monk's resolve if she put her mind to it. "I know where it is. Are you going to be able to find your way back to town okay?"

"Probably not." She grinned. "But don't worry. No matter how lost I get, I'll be there and waiting for you at seven. And I really appreciate your being willing to help me. Thanks again."

She flew toward the shiny red Civic before Pax could correct her—he had not, precisely, agreed to help her. He'd only agreed to talk a little further about her brother. And when push came to shove, he couldn't exactly remember even agreeing to that.

His gaze roamed the length of her—it didn't take long, not for a shrimp like her. Cute legs, but short. The color of her outfit was loud enough to wake a man from a sound sleep, and had some kind of sparkly appliqués on the front. The shorts and top hid nothing about her figure—no fanny to speak of, even though there was a hell of a swish in her walk, and not much on the upper deck, either. Her hair was the color of fire, and the blaze of curls tangled every which way around her face, no order, no control. With that vanilla-cream skin, he guessed her nose would be beet red by nightfall. And why the Sam Hill she'd be wearing long dangling earrings in the desert was beyond him.

There was no conceivable, justifiable, understandable reason why she had his blood pumping.

Pax had always liked women, and by thirty-two, he'd had the chance to know his share. Tall, leggy women were his preference, but he set no special stock in physical appearance. Temperament was more important. He sought out the women who liked the outdoors as much as he did, who were easygoing, natural to be with, restful.

Kansas McClellan was as restful as a rattlesnake.

He waited until she'd turned the rental car around before starting the Explorer's engine. He had a call to make after this—Juan Gonzalez's place—so he couldn't follow her all the way to town, but he could at least make sure she was steered toward the right road in the right county.

Pax grew up with some outmoded, archaic values about men protecting women. Whether or not he had a tolerance for ditsy, scatterbrained redheads was irrelevant. That particular redhead looked as frail and fragile as one of the rare, delicate blooms on a cactus, and everyone in the area knew that Pax had a long history of volunteering to help people in trouble. His motivation had never been largess, but more making up for the rough beginnings he'd had himself.

Without hearing more of the story, he wasn't sure he would—or could—help with the problem of finding her brother. But he'd suspicioned for some time that Case was dipping toward serious trouble. And he doubted that squirt of a lady could conceivably handle the kind of crowd her younger brother had gotten involved with—not without finding herself in some real danger.

She waved at him from the rearview mirror when she turned off at Hill Road. He watched her bump and bounce down the gravel road, driving way faster than was wise. Somehow he could have guessed she had a reckless lead foot. And for some reason he was again reminded of the hummingbirds who migrated to the canyons at this time of year; so tiny, so flashy and restless. But not at all as helpless as they appeared.

Abruptly he realized that his pulse was pumping adrenaline, as if some premonitory instinct were warning him to be careful about Kansas.

With a chuckle, he reached over to switch on the truck's radio. The lady was certainly interesting, but by no stretch of the imagination was she the kind of woman that he had ever been attracted to or involved with. Kansas was no danger to him. The thought was so humorous that he had to laugh.

Two

Kansas peered out the front window of her brother's place for the dozenth time: 6:50. Too early to worry that Pax wasn't going to show, yet her heart was still thudding with anxiety and nerves.

If Pax couldn't help find her brother, the world would not suddenly end. Kansas would find another way. She always had. But damn, right now she really didn't have a clue where else to turn.

Too antsy to sit still, she hustled into the bathroom to check her appearance. The mirror didn't reveal any noticeable difference since she checked five minutes ago. Her fresh-washed hair had been coaxed to look wilder with a judicious application of spritz. Exuberantly impractical bangles dangled from her wrists and ears. A filmy blouse covered a tank top, both tucked into her shorts with a jeweled belt. The blouse was emerald green and bright, but the fabric was as insubstantial as wind.

She looked—she hoped—like a helpless city slicker, inept, vulnerable, flighty, impractical…and momentarily she felt a qualm of conscience. It wasn't exactly *nice* to try to manipulate a man with her appearance. She'd only caught one weakness in Pax—a sense of honor as extinct as dinosaurs in most men. He had both a reputation and job that labeled him a rescuer. Never mind ethics. Her brother mattered more than any darn fool ethics, and if she looked like a woman who needed rescuing, it might up the odds of Pax being willing to help her.

Kansas slugged her hands into her shorts pockets, musing that the situation was downright humorous. She had a real bug about men who treated her like a helpless cookie. On the surface, it seemed the height of irony to be inviting the same response from Pax that drove her bananas. But life was more complicated than surface appearances, as Kansas had learned the hard, painful way.

Her mind inevitably spun back to the car accident. She'd been fourteen at the time, green-young, with a heart full of confident dreams about becoming a strong, athletic Amazon when she grew up. During those long months of recovery, it bit like a bullet to be a helpless invalid, hurt even more to be a dependent burden on those who loved her. En route, though, she'd discovered the difference between real pride and false pride.

She was never going to be a physically strong Amazon in this lifetime, but that measurement of strength had never been worth poppycock. Real strength—the kind of grit and guts that mattered—came from accepting whoever, or whatever you were. Just because a woman was stuck looking like a physical weakling never meant she couldn't be tougher than steel on the inside.

When Kansas heard the knock on the front door, her hand flew to her stomach. A woman of steel, she told herself firmly, should *not* be having a problem with jittery butterflies.

She sprinted for the door. When Pax walked in, she abruptly remembered where all those butterflies came from. Him. The toughest woman on earth could hardly fail to notice that he was one hormone-arousing hombre.

He'd cleaned up before coming over, and was dressed casually enough in jeans and a chambray shirt, but two of her could tuck in his shadow. His jet black hair was still damp from a recent shower, yanked back in a ponytail with a leather thong. Her pulse suddenly galloped around an electric racetrack. It wasn't something she could help. Personally she thought a man with eyes that dark, that deep should come with a warning about high voltage.

"Come on in. I appreciate your coming," she said cheerfully.

"I told you I would." He strode in, his posture as rigid as an oak trunk, but his gaze traveled the length of her. It didn't take him twenty seconds to make the journey from her city-slicker outfit to her wild baubles to her carrot-top artsy craftsy hairstyle. He noticeably relaxed, with an amused smile for her sunburned nose. "You look like you recovered from the heat this afternoon."

"Thankfully it cools down around here at night." She told herself she wasn't irked. An easy, relaxed smile was exactly what she wanted from Pax. Flash and sparkle were clearly not his personal cuppa, which was absolutely fine with her. She'd never dressed and fussed to have him notice her as a woman—she'd put on a version of the dog to win his sympathy for her brother's cause.

And Case, of course, was the only thing on her mind. She suddenly wrapped her arms tightly around her chest. "I've got some wine and crackers in the living room, but to be honest, I'd like to show you around first. I haven't had time to really clean the place up, so almost everything is just like I found it when I got here yesterday. I think I can show you why I'm so worried about my brother."

"I don't know that I can help you with your brother, Kansas."

"I know. I understand that. But I'm really coming into this area cold—I don't know anything. If nothing else, I'm hoping you could give me some leads or ideas."

"I'll try." His forehead suddenly creased in a frown. "For starters, was the house locked when you got here? How did you get in?"

Kansas could have told him that she'd climbed on two suitcases and broken in by jimmying a window latch with a crowbar. But somehow she didn't think Pax would be too quick to aid a helplessly impractical city slicker if she confessed such resourcefulness—or her willingness to commit breaking and entering without a single ethical qualm. ''The house *was* locked, which reassured me at first. I mean, it seemed to indicate that Case planned to be away. But then I got inside...''

She ushered him around, trying to show him the house as it had first appeared from her own eyes. Her brother had barely had two cents to rub together. The place he'd rented was a long way from deluxe—just four rooms, all simply done in adobe and tile.

The red-tiled kitchen was no bigger than a walk-in closet, with aging appliances and a jutting counter that functioned as an eating table. ''I *had* to clean up here. Case had left dirty dishes piled in the sink—which wasn't untypical of him—but the food was just crusted on. When I opened the refrigerator, there was spoiled milk, lunch meat that had turned prehistoric...'' She shook her head. ''Maybe he'd planned on going somewhere, but not for this long. Not for three weeks.''

''Case wasn't famous for planning ahead,'' Pax said pointedly.

''I know he's a little...impulsive. But he left so many other things just hanging.'' She jogged ahead. Just off the kitchen was a utility room, where an aging washing machine and dryer were located. She showed Pax how clothes had been left in the washer, dried out but never transferred to the dryer. And then she zoomed past him toward the only bathroom in the place, where basic men's toiletries were still strewn around the sink—toothpaste, shaving cream, razor, deodorant. "Everything he left is daily-life-necessity stuff—nothing he'd take for an evening, but positively things he would have packed if he'd planned on being gone for three weeks."

"I think you're right—the clues add up to a trip he didn't plan. But that still doesn't mean that Case disappeared in some frightening or scary sense, Kansas. He's just a kid, and few kids that age excel at responsible choices. He could easily have made a spur-of-the-moment decision to take off."

His voice reminded her of the nap side of velvet: soft, gentle, soothing. He probably calmed dozens of wounded critters with that sexy baritone, but it scraped against her feminine nerves like squeaky chalk. How was she ever going to get through to Pax if he persisted in being so logical?

"Maybe if I show you the bedroom," she said in frustration, and then stopped so quickly in the middle of the hall that Pax almost ran into her. "No. Forget the bedroom."

"Why?"

Because she had lingerie and clothes and her brand of "girl stuff" wildly strewn all through her brother's bedroom. Because she was oddly edgy around Pax without exposing an intimately unmade, rumpled bed to his dark eyes. "Because," she said, "there are just more important things to show you in the living room."

"Okay," he said, as gently as if he were talking to a skittery mouse.

She *felt* skittery. It wasn't just this increasingly strange feeling she had around Pax, but the attack of anxiety raising again about her brother. Something had happened to Case. She *knew* it. And walking into the living room intensified that restless feeling of worry and panic tenfold.

She gestured toward the pots of dead plants on the tile floor by the sliding glass doors. "You can see those plants wilted and died from lack of water…which, again, made me think that Case had never expected to be gone for so long. But those plants are so weird, besides…I mean, they look like ugly weeds, hardly some charming little philodendron or standard houseplant. And I can't imagine my brother taking the time to fuss with *any* plants—he never had a homemaker bone in his whole body. So that *really* struck me wrong, and then there was the letter—"

"What letter?"

She whisked around the worn tan couch and old, scarred bookcase. The living room was furnished with typical rental property decor—bland beiges and browns—so ordinary that she had no way to explain to Pax why the room first scared her. He couldn't know her brother. Not the way she did.

Case had always been more into playing than deep thinking—yet there were books about mysticism and religions and heavyweight philosophy stashed all over the bookshelves and tables. A stained-glass pentagram hung from one window; a Tibetan prayer wheel was stuck on a shelf. Maybe the previous renter had left them, because Kansas couldn't believe Case even knew what those symbols meant. The prints and posters tacked on the walls were all surreal unearthly scenes, wild and dark, and absolutely nothing like her brother's taste. At least the brother she knew.

But the most disturbing thing for Kansas was the letter. At the far corner of the living room was a battered pine desk, where she'd found the letter yesterday—a half-finished missive, to her, in Case's blunt scrawl and dated three weeks before. She picked up the white notebook paper, feeling such a huge well of anxiety that she could hardly swallow. "Case would *never* have left a half-finished letter. And it's to me. He mentions a girl, Serena—actually, he brought up her name before—but I have no idea what her last name is. And most of the letter is about how he finally found a way to turn his life around, something he was serious about and committed to...but that's when it ends. I don't know what he's talking about."

She spun around to hand Pax the letter, expecting him to be right behind her—but he hadn't followed her across the room. Instead he was hunkered down by the sliding doors, sniffing and then fingering the leaves of those long-dead plants.

"Do you know what those plants are?" she asked him.

"Yeah. I think so. It's a plant called datura. Common enough in the desert. Some call it jimsonweed."

"Why on earth would he grow a weed?" Kansas asked bewilderedly, and then sucked in a breath. "Don't tell me it's something like marijuana. I'd never believe you. My brother has faults—he can be wild and irresponsible and he doesn't always think things through—but at heart, he couldn't be more clean-cut. He was never the type to mess around with recreational drugs—"

"It's not an illegal substance, Kansas. Nor is it a recreational drug."

Since that was exactly what she wanted—and expected—to hear, Kansas should have felt reassured. Yet her heart suddenly seemed to be thudding louder than a base drum. Pax straightened, and then walked straight toward her and picked up the letter.

While he studied the letter, she studied him. Although Pax clearly wasn't a man to reveal emotion in his expressions, she sensed something had changed. Likely he had only made this visit because she'd played out the role of a lady in distress, not because he really believed her brother was in trouble.

But there was something dead quiet about the way he read that letter. And when he finished, he glanced back at the plants.

"What's wrong?" she asked. "You know something."

He hesitated. "I don't know anything, I told you. When Case first dropped in town, I ran into him in a restaurant. He had no place to bunk down, no money in his pockets. It was no hardship for me to give him a hand. He stayed with me for a short stretch, and I gave him part-time work in my surgery until he had some cash ahead. Then he found this place, got a job at a store in town. He stopped by to talk sometimes, shoot the bull. That's all, Kansas. I wasn't really in his confidence—''

''You know something,'' she repeated, her gaze on his face. ''What? Something about those plants?''

When he hesitated again, her instincts set off mental smoke alarms.

''Pax, for cripe's sake, you're scaring me half to death. If you have some idea where he is, what happened to him—''

''Like I said, I don't know anything...look, why don't we just sit down for a minute. I didn't mean to shake you up. I'll explain what I know. We'll just talk about this real calm, real quiet.''

''Okay,'' Kansas said. And on the catch of a breath, screamed at the top of her lungs.

Pax already had a few clues that Kansas was no more predictable than a loaded gun, but her sudden earsplitting scream came from absolutely nowhere. For such a sprite, she had a prize-winning set of lungs. And if the scream wasn't enough to stun him speechless, she suddenly threw herself straight into his arms.

He grabbed her. It wasn't a choice or thought, but just a basic, masculine physical response. The scream still ringing in his ears sounded petrified, and his instinctive reaction was to protect her. He'd have done the same thing for any other small, vulnerable creature—woman, child, animal, would have made no difference.

But in the spin of those seconds, Pax recognized a telling difference. Heat suddenly charged through his veins. Whatever scent she was wearing hit his nostrils with muscle-tightening awareness—no sweet, safe, flowery perfumes for Kansas, but something just like her: spicy and sensual and disturbingly unignorable.

She'd slammed into him with the force of a catapult—an awkward, miniature catapult. Her weight didn't throw him off-balance, but she did. Never mind her size. That small trembling body was still a woman's body, with a heart heaving like thunder and breasts layered so explicitly against him that every masculine hormone came stinging, singing awake. She had her arms cuffed so tightly around his waist that he couldn't breathe. For that millisecond, he didn't want to.

He wasn't expecting the jolt of chemistry. Not to her. Not with her. Even accounting for a stretch of abstinence, he'd never been remotely attracted to dynamite or trouble, and from his first glimpse, he'd sensed Kansas was both. Understanding his incomprehensible response to her would have to come later, though.

Her hair was stiff with mousse and tickled his chin; her dang fool shoulder-length earrings tangled with his collar—but over the top of her head, he abruptly spotted the reason for her scream. An extremely hairy orange and black tarantula was scooching slowly across the floor.

His heartbeat immediately simmered down and he almost laughed. Not at her fear, but at her response to the "avicularia." Kansas had already struck him as emotional and impulsive and pure female. Somehow he could have guessed that she'd never waste time on a halfway gasp when a full-body sissy scream would do.

"Kansas," he said gently, "it's just a spider."

"You call that a spider? I call it a monster—big enough to kill us both! How do you *live* in this horrible country? I'll never sleep for a week!"

"If you let me loose, I'll take care of it," he said soothingly.

"If you think I'm letting go of you, you're out of your mind!" But having made that completely irrational statement, she reared back her head and shrieked again when she saw the tarantula.

By tomorrow, maybe, his ears might stop ringing. "I'm not saying you want to be bitten by one, but it's not going to attack you. If you just calm down for two seconds—"

"Calm down? I hate spiders and crawly things! Oh, God, oh, God. I'm gonna have nightmares about this for a year!"

Pax opened his mouth to try to reassure her again—and abruptly and completely closed his mouth.

Kansas, still ranting, tore loose from his arms. Still raving about how petrified she was, she raced across the room and grabbed a folded newspaper. Still claiming to be an ace-pro wuss who couldn't handle, just couldn't handle, creepy-crawly critters, she scooped the tarantula onto the paper, whisked across the room to open the sliding doors and let the critter outside.

When she slammed the glass door closed, she leaned against it with a dramatic hand on her chest. "I think I'm gonna have a heart attack."

Pax scratched his chin. He'd thought she was going to have a heart attack, too. He would have quickly educated her about how painful a tarantula bite could be—if she'd given him the chance. He would also have taken care of the critter for her—if she hadn't moved at the speed of light and done it herself.

For someone who made big noises about being a self-proclaimed coward and a gutless wimp, Kansas wasn't quite living up to her image.

Or maybe she just wasn't what she seemed.

Kansas suddenly peered up at him. "You probably think I'm a scatterbrained ditz."

That thought *had* crossed his mind. "Actually it's a pretty good idea to be scared of tarantulas...and the same goes for a few other desert critters who live around here. Most have a far more exaggerated reputation than they deserve, but a tarantula bite can hurt real good. Best to stay away from them."

"I'll be happy to." She clawed a hand through her hair, which made a cowlick stick up in a spike. "I'm gonna have the willies all night unless I check every corner of the house for any more of those things."

Pax could have offered. It wasn't a lack of chivalry that kept him silent, but just plain dark humor. Kansas kept saying how terrified she was, but she certainly didn't seem to be counting on anyone to rescue her. A man might even come to the confounded conclusion that the lady was damn used to rescuing herself. He glanced again at the ethereal blouse, the fragile bones, the sky-soft blue eyes, the impractical baubly jewelry dangling and tangling all over the place...

"Pax—do you want some wine or something? Before that tarantula scared the wits out of me, I thought you were going to tell me something about my brother."

"I'm not much on wine." He glanced at his watch. "And it's getting pretty late. I've got a call on a rancher at six in the morning."

Immediately she looked guilty. "I didn't mean to take so much of your time."

"Hey, I volunteered." More to the point, Pax just wasn't sure what to say about her brother. Long before Kansas arrived, he'd had some suspicions clawing in his mind about what Case might have gotten himself involved with. The things she'd showed him around the place had worried him more.

But suspicions weren't fact. And even if his worries were true, Pax still wasn't sure what or how to tell Kansas anything. No question, she had a lioness's fierce loyalty to her brother. That was a sweet quality, a damn fine quality that Pax only wished someone had felt toward him in his own life. But to let an emotional, impulsive sissy of a city baby loose in a situation way out of her ken—hell, Kansas could land herself in a heap of trouble, if not downright danger.

She walked him to the front door with her arms wrapped around her chest and her mouth zipped in a firm line. No talking. She respected that it was late and he had to leave. Her gaze kept shooting to his face, though, and Pax had the uneasy feeling that she'd rope and hog-tie him if he dared try leaving without saying something else about Case.

When he pushed open the back door, she was as faithful as a dog on his heels. It had turned dark. The lights of Sierra Vista were a soft glow in the sky to the north, but this far out of town, there were no lights, no traffic, no people noise. The night came alive here. The air was impossibly clear and pure, the silence soothing on a man's soul. So typically, the Arizona spring night was seeped in desert smells and sounds and a huge, ghost white full moon—his favorite kind.

Kansas's gaze was still glued tightly on his face. Pax doubted she noticed the moon or the night—at that precise moment, he doubted she'd notice an earthquake—and mentally sighed. Yeah, he'd been thinking about the problem of her brother.

"My work schedule is pretty weird," he told her. "I'm not an 'office hours' kind of vet. About the only thing I do in the office is surgery—most of my work is out in the field, and I use a cellular phone for people trying to track me down. My hours are always crazy, and like I said, I really don't know where your brother is, Kansas. The best I could do—if you don't mind working around my hit-or-miss schedule—is take you around, show you some places where Case used to go, that kind of thing."

"That kind of thing would be *wonderful,*" she said fervently, and smiled like he'd just turned on the switch for the sun. "That was all I was asking for—some help. I know it's an imposition, and I really appreciate the offer. In fact I would be glad to pay you—"

"Around here, we haven't caught up with big city values yet. A neighbor still helps a neighbor. Money has nothing to do with it." Pax dug the truck key out of his jeans pocket. He doubted the wisdom of getting involved, but there was no help for it. Letting Kansas poke and pry on her own just wouldn't sit on his conscience. "I won't be free tomorrow until after three in the afternoon."

"That'd be great."

Pax wasn't sure it'd be great. He wasn't sure of anything except that he felt a whomp upside the head every time he looked at her.

Kansas moved aside so he could open the driver's door to the Explorer. He opened the door, but he didn't immediately climb in.

It had been a long time since anyone or anything confused him. His real name, Paxton, had been shortened to Pax because the Latin base for the nickname had always pegged his personality.

He liked peace. He'd had enough turmoil in his childhood to last forever. Most things that mattered in life reduced to simple terms, if a man was determined to lead a simple life.

Nothing seemed simple about Kansas. Right then, she was standing in a shower of moonlight, her eyes softer than the big black sky. The filmy blouse she wore was no thicker than a veil, and never mind that it was sexier than a man's midnight fantasies. The fabric was ethereal and fragile, and everything she wore, every damn thing she did, shouted loudly that she was a wimp and a wuss and a crushably vulnerable woman.

Yet she'd taken off cross-country without a qualm "to save" her brother. And he'd watched the confounded shrimp tackle the tarantula, when she had a rescuer right at her fingertips who could have handled it. It didn't make sense. *She* didn't make sense.

Kansas cocked her head. "I'm in no rush if you want to stand here all night," she murmured humorously. "But you're looking at me like there's a bug on my nose."

"There's no bug on your nose."

"Maybe you were thinking of something else having to do with my brother? Because if there's anything else you could tell me about Case—"

"I wasn't thinking about your brother." Pax

just kept thinking that somehow, someway, he had to figure out what kind of woman Kansas really was.

She could get hurt if he misjudged what she was capable of.

She could get into serious trouble unless he had a measure of what she could handle—and what she couldn't.

All Pax wanted was some simple, clean-cut answers. In a dozen years, though—in a hundred years—he never planned on kissing her.

Three

Kansas didn't move when he took a step toward her. And she saw his arm reach up, felt the knuckles of his hand brush her cheek. But Pax didn't seem to even be thinking about her. There was a dark wedge of a frown grooved in his brow, as if some weighty problem was consuming his attention.

Even when he ducked his head, it just never occurred to her that he planned to kiss her. There'd been no come-on. No man-woman exchange of looks or body-language signals. If anything, Kansas sensed that Pax saw her as a pesky little sister—humorous and a little annoying, but as safe as a sibling to be with.

His lips touched hers, in a whispery-soft kiss. A safe kiss. A kiss swifter than the feather stroke of a spring wind.

Her heartbeat picked up a sudden, strange rhythm, but she still didn't move. Even if the kiss was a surprise, no threat of danger crossed her mind. Heaven knew what motivated Pax to kiss her at all, but she had no fear of where it was going. Every man she'd ever known had treated her like breakable china. It wasn't their fault; positively her delicate appearance provoked that attitude, but her looks were nothing she could change. Still, she was so experienced at handling careful, cautious, gentle kisses that she never anticipated any other kind.

His hands sieved into her hair and he tilted her face up. His black eyes burned on her face for all of a second, before his mouth dipped down again.

Holy kamoly. For damn sure he wasn't kissing his sister this time.

Fire shot through her veins before she'd even smelled sulphur. The shock alone curled her toes. Pax wasn't trapping her—except for his big hands framing her face, he wasn't holding her at all. The only connection was his smooth, warm lips tasting hers, then taking hers, with a pressure that made her blood spin.

Reflexively her hands shot up. Her fingers closed around his wrists, not necessarily to stop him. Just to hold on. She sure as patooties needed something to hold onto, because an innocuously pale moonlit night had abruptly exploded with color.

He was supposed to treat her like a fragile cookie. Everyone else did. Every other man had always kissed her...respectfully. Pax kissed her like someone had accidentally opened the cage doors on a big, hungry bear—a bear who'd been contained and deprived of sustenance for just too long. She couldn't catch her breath. He seemed to have the same problem.

His shadow covered her more completely than a sheet on a bed. She couldn't see his face, but she could feel the harsh, beating pulse in his wrists, hear the raw, rough sound that came out of his throat. It was a lonely sound. Lonely and wild. And he sealed her mouth under his with the pressure of a brand. His brand.

He was a relative stranger, her mind recognized, and Kansas hadn't survived to the vast age of twenty-nine without knowing the girls' rule book. When a stranger came on to a woman with the intimidating force of a steamroller, she wasn't supposed to melt faster than ice cream in the tropics. She was supposed to sock him. She was supposed to make him behave. And if those options weren't clear-cut easy, she was supposed to have the good sense to run faster than the wind.

But she didn't run. And when his tongue found hers, an unprincipled kiss that was already pushing the boundaries of trouble suddenly dived straight off that cliff. He tasted dark and wicked. He tasted exotic and forbidden. He tasted like the most dangerous flavor she'd ever tried...yet her fingers loosened on his wrists, hovered for a second in midair, and then slowly wrapped tightly around his waist.

Her response wasn't something she could justify, not in rational terms. Yet her never-too-logical heart seemed to think she'd known Pax forever. Maybe one tough, strong cookie recognized another. Maybe it took someone who'd never belonged to anything or anyone, to recognize how fierce and desperate that longing could be in someone else.

There were no maybes on her mind at that instant, just emotions taking her under with gale force. She kissed him back, as she'd never dared kiss anyone. She took him in, as if a pipsqueak-size woman could actually shelter a tall, strong man in the circle of her arms. Some need in Pax touched her heart. And damnation, no one had ever touched her heart, not like this.

Her feet arched up on tiptoe. Her breasts tightened, arched, ached against his chest. His belt buckle grazed her abdomen. The angle of stark moonlight on his face, the warmth pouring off his skin, the tight flex of his thighs and the shiver-arousing feeling of his arousal growing, pressed intimately between them—if she had been more razor-sharp aware of a man, she didn't know when. She could feel his whole body shudder with tension—sexual tension that had suddenly become as volatile as lightning.

Kansas kept telling herself she should be scared—maybe even scared out of her mind—but she'd never known this crazy kind of heat even existed. If this was madness and mayhem, she'd been waiting for it all her life. Damned if she'd be afraid of something this rich, this wondrous and powerful. And damned if there'd ever been a man who'd made her feel this way. Liquid from the inside out. Needed. Desired. As if nothing else existed but the two of them at that pure moment in time.

It didn't last. On a harsh groan, he tore his mouth free and reared his head back. Firm hands grasped her by the shoulders and forced a separation. His lungs hauled in air like he'd been underwater for the last year or two.

If putting some physical distance between them was supposed to cool him down, or calm him down, it didn't seem to be working. His eyes looked dazed drunk in the moonlight. He looked at her, and then hauled in another lungful of air. "Kansas...I didn't mean that to happen. Hell. I don't even know *what* happened."

Her relationship with gravity was still a little shaky, and she was having the same tough time catching her breath as he was. Still, she definitely didn't share his problem with figuring out what happened. He'd kissed the living socks off her. And she'd kissed him back the same way. "It's all right," she said gently.

"The hell it is. I'm sorry."

"There's nothing to be sorry for."

"Yeah, there is. I don't...I would never have...hell," he said again, and clawed a hand at the back of his neck. "I apologize for jumping you. And I don't want you afraid that it'll happen again. It won't.''

Kansas realized fleetingly that Pax was rattled. She rattled easily—didn't take any more than a mouse running across the floor—but she suspicioned that Pax rarely let his control off the leash. He didn't seem to know where to look, what to say, or what the Sam Hill he was supposed to do. And she was afraid it might go on forever—his swallowing hard and saying hell in between apologies—unless she took charge.

''Hey, there's no problem here,'' she said calmly. ''Maybe I was surprised when you kissed me. Maybe we were both surprised. But people have been indulging in that particular pastime since the beginning of time...'' Oops, she thought that might earn a smile, but no. ''No one's upset, right? No one's mad. Everybody's fine. And it's late, like you said. Let's just call it a night, and I'll see you tomorrow.''

He leaped on that excuse to split, she noticed dryly, like a dog for a bone. Moments later, the Explorer's headlights bounced out of her driveway.

She headed inside, intending to lock up, clean up and get ready for bed. She locked up, then completely forgot the rest of that game plan, and found herself standing in the front window, staring out at the empty driveway.

Her heart was beating like a revved up 747.

Thoughts were tumbling through her mind like dandelion fluff in a hurricane wind.

And every feminine hormone in her body was alive, awake and singing arias.

Inappropriate arias, Kansas mused. It was only a kiss. From a man who clearly wished he hadn't indulged in the impulse, and in a place where she neither lived nor planned to stay long. As there was positively no chance to pursue a relationship, there was absolutely nothing to worry about.

And she wasn't worried. She'd just never felt that fierce, instantaneous pull for anyone else. Before completely giving up men—which, as far as Kansas was concerned, was the most brilliant decision she ever made—she was no stranger to passion. Hal had been her last lover, and making love with him had been nice. Messy and time-consuming, but nice. Maybe she had an unusual pocketful of inhibitions, but she'd never been in a tearing hurry to get naked with a man, and Hal had been sweet, gentle, comfortable. Untenably, exasperatingly, as possessive as a bloodhound, but the intimate side of their relationship had been A-OK. She'd thought.

How startling, to discover at the vast age of twenty-nine, that a man could wipe all those previous preconceptions right off the map. If Pax had scared her, it was the most delicious scared she could remember. No man had ever kissed her like a lush slide straight into sensual oblivion, as if her whole world had been an arid desert until he touched her.

Kansas wasn't about to mistake a molehill for a mountain—for both of them, it had probably just been a crazy, lost moment in time.

But she didn't want to forget that kiss.

Kansas turned around, and forced her mind to concentrate on getting ready for bed. She had a bad, bad feeling that falling for Pax could be a terrible temptation. That wouldn't do at all; not for him or her. For a few moments there, she'd almost forgotten that she was violently, sensibly and firmly off men.

It was a relief to remember that.

Pax turned down Cactus Court with a glance at the digital clock on his dash. Three o'clock on the button.

It was going to be a lot easier to deal with

Kansas, he considered, now that he knew for sure she was a stark-raving lunatic.

His experience with her the night before couldn't possibly have been more helpful. He had her measure now. She might be a wimp, but she had more guts—and recklessness—than any twenty women. And before getting any further involved in her brother's problem, that was precisely what Pax needed to know—how she'd respond to trouble.

Now he knew.

She had no concept of trouble or danger at all. Skydive without a parachute—no problemo for Kansas. Pet a grizzly bear—what fun. Respond to a guy she barely knew with open vulnerability and passion and a free, naked invitation to do whatever the hell he wanted...*damn* that woman. Had she even *thought* about saying no?

Pax braked in her driveway, and slammed the door as he leaped out of the Explorer. Hot sun beat down on his shoulders, healing, soothing sun. He'd been up since five. Spring was calving season. He'd showered before leaving the Hernandez ranch—most of the local ranchers offered him a meal and a place to clean up as an automatic courtesy. So he was clean, but his muscles still ached from the physical work and long, grueling hours. He wouldn't have minded ten minutes to put his feet up.

He'd have been even happier if the memory of Kansas coming apart in his arms would disappear, splat, from his mind. And yeah, he was guilty of initiating that kiss. But he'd only intended a kiss, not a pass. He'd only intended to test her a little, see how she responded to a little surprise, a little stress. God knew how it had gotten out of hand so fast.

It was *her* fault. Completely. Only blaming her somehow didn't make him feel better. Pax did not open up to strangers. Ever. He positively did not come onto women like a rabid bull. Ever. He was a grown man, a hundred years too old to let hormones rule his life or his behavior, and he had never touched a woman where he wasn't in full control. It was unconscionable. It couldn't have happened.

The front door hurled open...and Pax mentally braced. Trouble bounced outside, in a flurry of ditsy chitchat and a wincing bright orange streak of color.

''Hi there, Pax! You're right on time. Wait, wait, wait—I forgot my purse...and I'd better lock the door. I just have to remember where I put the key to the house....''

Pax wiped a hand over his face as he waited for her to shoot back inside and come up with the key and purse and heaven knew what else. Last night *must* have been some kind of surreal fantasy, something he'd half imagined or blown out of proportion in his mind. This was the Kansas he'd first met. One of those alien species known as a Pure Female. In her case, a pure ditsy female, a chatterer with just an eensy tendency to be an airhead.

She chased back outside with a grin bigger than the sky, a floppy crocheted bag dangling from her arm. Her fingers were covered—plastered—in rings; bracelets clattered around her wrists; and he hadn't a clue how to classify what she was wearing. Technically it seemed to be some kind of dress, but it buttoned from a loose neck and ended midthigh. A short midthigh. The fabric was a light cotton knit, and snuggled up to every skinny bone. Hell, a gusty sigh would probably knock her down.

Her fragility hit him every time he saw her. Never mind all the flash and sparkle—he'd felt her body last night. She didn't own a sturdy bone and her skin was softer than a baby's behind. He guessed she'd bruise if a man even looked at her roughly, and that thought was disturbing. Pax couldn't imagine her surviving in any physically demanding situation—past five minutes—and there was just no way this side of the moon that he could stop himself from feeling protective of her.

"Ready," she announced, and gave him another winsome, wicked grin. "At least I think I'm ready. We didn't exactly pin down an agenda for the afternoon. Do we have a game plan on the table about where we're going?"

"I have a place in mind, where your brother used to spend some time. But first—I should have asked you yesterday if you'd talked to the sheriff."

"Why, sure. When I couldn't get ahold of Case and started worrying he was missing, the first places I called were the hospitals—and then the law. Sheriff Simons and I are old phone pals. I called him at least a half dozen times from Minnesota."

"And?"

"And...he was real sweet and real kind, but all those long-distance calls got me nowhere." Kansas climbed into the passenger side of the Explorer and strapped herself in.

His Explorer was used to smelling like hay and vet medicines and a whole host of other natural, earthy smells. But his truck, for sure, had never been exposed to a blast of exuberantly sexy French perfume. Something about that audacious scent—or her—was developing a dangerous habit of arousing his hormones. But Pax consoled himself that at least she'd made no reference to the kiss the night before. Apparently they were both going to play this nice and comfortable and pretend it never happened—which was totally okay by him.

"The sheriff went so far as to drive out to Case's place," Kansas continued. "But when he didn't find any sign of breaking in or a problem, he said that was the best he could do. There was no reason to think my brother was really missing. Case had a habit of taking off on any whim, and apparently everyone around here knew it. Unless I come up with some reason or proof that Case is in trouble, the sheriff just said he had no legal basis to do anything."

"I told you the same thing yesterday," Pax reminded her.

"Yeah, I know you did." Blue eyes skimmed his face, then zipped away. "That's exactly why I'm grateful that you believed me."

"I don't necessarily believe that your brother is in trouble," he said, correcting her.

"He is." Her voice had turned quiet. "And you must believe me to some extent, or you wouldn't be here."

That wasn't precisely true. Pax checked the rearview mirror and backed out of the driveway. "*Al loco y al aire, darles calle,*" he murmured under his breath.

"Pardon?"

"It's a common Spanish saying around here. Clear the way for madmen and the wind." Pax didn't mention that men usually pounced on that Southwestern proverb in reference to the insanity of arguing with a stubborn woman. If he hadn't been afraid Kansas would take off on her own—and potentially risk running into trouble—he wouldn't be here.

"Madmen...?" she repeated curiously.

"It's nothing. Just a thought that crossed my mind." He switched subjects quickly. "There's a place at the far end of Sierra Vista. Just a bookstore, with a kind of deli and coffee shop attached. Doesn't sound like anything, but somehow the kids have made it into a hangout spot. I know Case used to spend a lot of time there."

"Great."

Pax couldn't swear that it would be "great"—or that Kansas would gain any helpful leads there about her brother. But it seemed a relatively safe place to start. His mind zipped back to the image of the datura plants at her place. It wasn't a good omen, those plants. "Tell me about your brother," Pax suggested.

"Tell you about Case? What do you want to know?" Adobe buildings with red-tiled roofs flashed by. The landscape was dominated by signs in Spanish and native cactus lying dusty in the sun. She kept looking out the window as if the view were as alien as a visit to the moon.

Pax loved his town. Sierra Vista was peaceful, quiet, clean and sleepy, even midafternoon downtown. Negotiating a little traffic didn't inhibit him from stealing glances at her. "I think it takes a hell of a loyal sister to just fly down on nothing more than a hunch that her brother may or may not be in trouble. Didn't you have to leave a job?"

"Yeah. I work in an art store in Minneapolis, close to the campus for the college of art and design. I frame pictures, work on displays, that kind of thing. But no one's real rigid about work schedules. Taking off for a couple weeks was no problem, as long as I could afford to do it without pay. I had some money saved, and my living expenses were never high. I live in a loft—the attic of this wonderful old three-story house—and the rent is wonderfully inexpensive.''

''A loft,'' he echoed, and mentally sighed. From her crazy jewelry and wild clothes, he could have guessed her artsy-craftsy background. It was no stretch at all to picture her living in some ''romantic'' artist's loft, surrounded by a pile of impractical, ethereal dreamers for friends.

''Actually it wouldn't have mattered if I had the money to afford this trip or not. Case is my brother.'' To Kansas, that seemed to say everything. ''He was there for me when I was little. The ten-year age span between us never mattered. There was a period when I went through some real hard times. Case was always in my corner.''

''What kind of hard times?'' Pax asked swiftly. He sensed the answer mattered, that it was a serious clue to understanding Kansas—and maybe her brother, too. But she sidestepped the question smoother than a Las Vegas showgirl, and kicked right back to the subject of Case.

''He had trouble in school, was diagnosed as ADD—attention deficit disorder—around the junior high years. Case was smart. He just couldn't settle down, couldn't concentrate. Medication helped some, but it was easy for the school system to peg him as trouble. And since he was full of the devil, he seemed to feel obligated to live up to that reputation.''

''I think there's a slim chance that a little... spirit runs in your family.''

''You can take that one to the bank.'' She chuckled her agreement, yet her tone abruptly turned serious again. ''He never did anything really wrong, Pax. No trouble with the law, no vandalism or drugs or drinking or anything like that. The things he did were just...mischief. Staying out late. Skipping classes. He wasn't allergic to work, just never had any specific ambition that took his interest. And he's such a life lover. He's higher than a kite over a sunny day or a tromp in the woods—anything at all—and he makes everyone around him feel just as good.''

''You don't have to sell me, Kansas. I believe you. I knew him. He's a happy-go-lucky charmer. Everyone around here liked him on sight.''

''I just wanted to be sure you knew—there isn't a bad bone in his whole body.''

Pax privately concurred in that personality assessment of her brother, but would have shut up, even if he hadn't. A she-wolf protecting her cub had nothing on Kansas. Pax had never had an advocate in his corner, within or outside a family; couldn't even remember a time when he didn't have to take care of himself.

"My Lord," she said suddenly.

"What?" He'd pulled into the strip mall parking lot and just thrown the Explorer in park.

"You said a bookstore. I figured you meant a Dalton's or Waldenbooks or something like that."

"No," Pax said, "this isn't exactly the kind of bookstore where you run in to buy a *Popular Mechanics* or pick up a paper." Two Harleys were parked at the curb, and several other breeds of black-and-chrome bikes were parked down the way. The sign over the door said Food For The Spirit. Crystals and charms hung from the display window, and the nest of books advertised up front had pictures of spirits and ghosts and "other world" symbols.

Pax pocketed the truck key, climbed out of the Explorer and met up with Kansas at the storefront. "I can't guarantee you'll pick up any information about your brother here. For one thing, I'm just not sure you'll get anyone to talk. This crowd isn't big on chitchatting with strangers. All I can tell you is that I know Case spent a lot of time here."

"Oh, I'll get them to talk, not to worry," Kansas murmured, and flashed him a smile.

He'd have smiled back, if his heartbeat hadn't suddenly stopped dead. For reasons he couldn't fathom, she was loosening another button at the neckline of her dress. Even accounting for Kansas's unpredictability—and the heat—it seemed a hell of a time to strip.

With that button undone, the fabric gaped like an open window on a magnolia white throat with a spray of freckles. No man could have ignored the distracting path of those freckles. Kansas swiftly fluffed her hair, and then just as swiftly adopted a posture with her arms hugged tight under her chest. The mess she'd made of her hair made her look just-out-of-bed sexy. The hugging-herself gesture made her look small and defenseless...and dammit, she was showing off that vulnerably flat chest.

Pax wanted to shake his head in bewilderment. It was like watching Hyde turn into Jekyll. A minute ago, they'd been having a sensible, serious conversation. She was bright. And insightful. The strength of her loyalty to her brother said a lot about her character and values. And damned if he could figure out how—in the course of a few seconds—she could transform back into the image of a crushably vulnerable wimp.

"You ready to go in, Pax?"

Kansas had shot ahead of him and already reached the door. It seemed that he'd looked dead when he'd been staring so hard at her. He hiked—fast—to her side.

"Let's hit it," he said, and pulled open the door. The wimp ducked under his arm and zipped into the store. Pax washed a hand over his face, feeling confounded and vaguely alarmed.

This little outing was supposed to be real simple.

Somehow he had the disastrous feeling it wasn't going to turn out that way.

Four

"I'm so glad you were willing to talk with me. I felt so...alone. I just had nowhere to turn."

Pax cuffed a chin in his palm. A cup of cappuccino sat cooling in front of him. He was thirsty enough, but hated to spare a minute to drink it. He'd never seen a con artist at work before.

Kansas was laying it on thicker than the residue on a horse racetrack. Her victim was a wild-haired, barrel-chested, tattooed young man with a gold ring in his eyebrows—weighing about 220 pounds, Pax guessed. The lad's appearance was intimidating enough to make any normal woman either run for cover or a weapon. Kansas was treating him like an adorable puppy, and so far, Mr. Muscle Bound couldn't seem to stop himself from drooling.

"Once you said you were Case's sister, I knew you had to be okay. And like, hey, man, you don't have to tell me what it's like to feel alone. I been there."

"Oh, George, I just knew you'd understand. And I've just been so upset about my brother. When I got here and couldn't find him...gee, I just didn't know what to do. Case and I...well, both of us always seemed to beat to a different drummer."

"Oh man, do I ever know exactly where you're coming from. You do something a little different, believe something a little different, and the whole world just climbs all over your case like you committed a crime."

"Lord, I know." She smiled at the slugger winsomely, and laid her ringed hand affectionately on his beefy wrist. "It sounds like you knew my brother really well. And I wouldn't put you on the spot for anything. Case is a private person, too. He wouldn't talk to just anyone about..."

She hesitated delicately. Pax had never seen

anyone fish for a shark with nothing more for bait than a minnow and a wild guess, but Mr. Beefcake shot a wary look around the room, then focused a baleful stare right at him.

Kansas said swiftly, "Pax is a friend. We can trust him."

"Yeah?" George didn't look convinced, but Kansas's slim hand squeezing his seemed to distract him. Two hundred twenty pounds of puddle—a disgrace to the entire male species—gazed right into her eyes. "A lot of people get real nervous about the group. Can't talk to just anyone. They don't understand."

"But I do, George...although, without knowing if you were part of that group with Case..." Kansas hesitated again. Another hook thrown out, big ocean, and Pax knew damn well she couldn't have a clue what she was fishing for.

"Well, I gotta say, I wasn't that close. Never got that big involved like your brother is. Man, that religious stuff gets real complicated, just not my thing. But I'm cool with what they were doing. To each their own karma, you know?"

Pax kept an ear open, listening to every sliver of information she weaned out of her prey. He hadn't been positive what Case was involved in. But he'd guessed. And the logical calculator in the back of his mind was punching buttons, adding up every obscure clue Mr. Beefcake let slip, hoping some answers would emerge about whatever action needed to be taken about Case.

What needed to be done about Kansas seemed a more complicated problem.

Pax glanced around. A curtain of beads separated the coffee shop from the otherworld bookstore. The whole place was dark on the inside, with lung-choking incense creating more smoke than the smokers. A bearded kid was mumbling poetry in the far corner. Love charms were for sale behind the counter, as were tapes of Gregorian chants and crystals promising to boost one's connection with one's deep inner spirit. No one in the store was over twenty-five, with the exception of Kansas and him. Pax had no doubt about his own maturity.

Hers was a real iffy question.

She kept batting her lashes at Tiger. She didn't have any lashes to bat, except those short skinny reddish ones. She kept leaning forward, so the fabric of her *damn* skimpy dress pressed tight against her chest. She didn't have any chest to toot. The whispery voice and I'm-so-helpless big eyes was a routine she shouldn't have been able to sell at the circus. George was as turned on as a buck in rutting season.

And dammit, so was he. Pax gulped down a

swallow of cappuccino, hoping for a jolt of reality, wishing to hell he had a dictionary to define her. She was trying to get information, and from a stranger who clearly didn't want to talk with her initially. He understood that. Never mind if he wanted to button up that damn dress and cover the rest of her throat with a big, thick scarf. It wasn't her using her sexy, skinny body as a distraction to get information that bothered him. At least not much.

It was her.

Sometimes everyone had to walk into tough situations, tangle with the unfamiliar and handle problems that could not be anticipated or prepared for. But when a man was at a disadvantage, he put his chin up and straightened his shoulders. Pax had learned the rules of surviving when he was knee high—you showed strength. You never showed weakness. Revealing your underbelly to a stranger gave someone else the power to hurt you.

Kansas was not only parading her weaknesses, but she was also showing them off. Deliberately. Flaunting to that overgrown beefcake that she was helpless and alone...hell, it was enough to give Pax an ulcer, and he'd always had an unruffably calm, easygoing nature. They were gonna be lucky if they escaped this place without

George making a pass. And yeah, he was there. No harm was going to come to her—nobody was gonna lay a finger on her—but *damn* the dimwit woman. What if he hadn't been there? Could she really blindly, blithely invite this kind of trouble when she was loose on her own?

"George," she said sometime later, "you've been such an enormous sweetie."

Pax doubted that George had ever been called a sweetie in his lifetime—even by his mother—and the brawny lad blushed straight through his rag tail whiskers. He also followed them to the door, as faithful as a puppy that was begging to be taken home.

Once both men were standing, though, it wasn't hard to exert some take-charge control in the situation. George was muscle-bound, but Pax was six foot two and hard fit from a physical lifestyle. George was a boy. Pax was a man. A little tactful eye contact effectively communicated those messages. George didn't follow them any farther than the door.

A hot, desert wind was blowing from the west when they stepped outside. Sand blurred the air, softening the sharp edges on all the man-made structures, dusting man's harsh colors. Kansas pelted for the truck, as if the wind would bite her, and climbed in.

''How can you breathe in this dust?'' she muttered as she yanked on the seat belt, and then said, ''Oh, God, Pax. He scared me half to death. There's some kind of religious cult around here, isn't there? That was what he was talking about? In a thousand years, I'd never have guessed my brother could be involved in something like that.''

''You don't know that he is, for sure.'' Pax turned the key in the ignition, but his eyes honed on her. Damned if she wasn't Kansas again. Gone was the silly batting eyelashes business and the waif-vulnerable expression. She dragged a hand through her hair, making it stand up in spikes...and for reasons he couldn't—or wouldn't—understand, hormones soared through his blood in a zinging rush of desire.

He remembered what happened last night when he'd given in to the impulse to kiss her. And ordered his eyes on the road.

''No, I don't know for sure,'' she admitted, ''but that's increasingly what it sounds like. And now I'm remembering all those books on alternative religions at the house. The books, the strange pictures, all the clutter Case has around. And the people in that store. They're just babies, for pete's sake. Kids.''

''George,'' Pax informed her, ''was no kid.''

Kansas waved off that opinion with a hand gesture. "I don't care if he was a teenager or in his twenties. He was still a kid. No experience in life, no judgment."

"Kansas," Pax tried again, his tone as tactful as he could make it, "he was old enough to have sex on his mind—and big enough to give you a seriously hard time if he'd made a pass."

"For heaven's sakes, that was never going to happen. He must have noticed that I was at least five years older than him."

Pax sighed. Heavily.

"Anyway, George has nothing to do with anything," Kansas said fretfully, and dragged a wild hand through her hair again. "The point is this 'group' he kept referring to. Do you know who this group is? Or specifically what kind of religion he was eluding to?"

"There've been rumors about a cult," Pax said carefully, "but no one knows anything for positive. All kids look for places to hang out. Originally the group that took up at that bookstore were clean-cut and as straight as arrows—nothing in physical appearance like George. Like most kids, they were looking for a cause. The initial group was big on the environment, natural foods, conservation—and moaning about everything this generation has done to muck up the environment."

"Well, that doesn't sound so weird. And I can easily believe that kind of thing would interest Case."

Pax nodded, but he was still careful about choosing his words. "I think it's pretty natural that kids, coming from that attitude, would be drawn to some of the early Native American religions and beliefs. There are some strong ideals in the old ways. Compelling, idealistic beliefs. Our Native people were a lot smarter about the earth than whites and other races ever were."

"But...?" Kansas prodded him.

"But ideas like mysticism and shamans and psychic experiences can sound real romantic to a kid, especially if they're taken out of context and he's only being presented with one part of the picture. A lot of grounds for potential trouble there. Misinterpretation. It's real easy to end up down a side road that's a long, long way from the original highway of ideas you started out with."

"What are they up to? What are you trying to tell me?"

"I'm not trying to tell you anything. Case was taken with that crowd. That's the only real fact I know."

''Facts!'' Kansas said disparagingly, as if anything so logical were beyond all relevance. ''Well, I'm going to find out more. That's for sure. I'm going to find my brother, and I'm going to get to the bottom of this, and I don't care what I have to do—''

''Kansas...'' Pax had to interrupt her. Alarm bells were shooting acid to his stomach. All it took was a vision of a pint-size redhead playing vigilante all on her lonesome. ''Don't you dare go off on your own.''

''I beg your pardon?''

Aw, hell. He never meant that to sound like an order. ''I just meant...if you want to look for your brother, I'll help you. I know the area, the people, the places, which you can't possibly be familiar. It would take you forever if you tried to do it alone.''

''It would,'' she agreed, and then said softly, ''thanks. It's a huge relief to know I can count on you.''

Counting on him, Pax thought grimly, had nothing to do with it. There was a saying in the Southwest. *Bien sabe el diablo a quien se le aparece.* The devil will take advantage of anyone he can intimidate—or in more prosaic terms—the more vulnerable in life were always going to be prey.

In principle, it wasn't his responsibility to protect Kansas. But there simply was no one else in any conceivable position to volunteer for the job.

Kansas fell silent on the drive, trying to absorb the disturbing information she'd picked up about her brother and strategize what she could do about it. Until Pax pulled in her driveway, though, she hadn't realized that he'd fallen into a pensive silence, too.

Without a word, he climbed out of the Explorer and strode around to her side of the truck. Broad daylight, Kansas mused, yet Pax still considered it automatic to open a woman's door and walk her to the house.

Personally she'd always been thrilled chivalry was dead, because every man she knew with a protective streak had never *really* been protective. They'd been possessive. Maybe they didn't know the difference, but Kansas was slowly picking up the unique idea that Pax did. The strong protected those who were less strong. It seemed to be the code he lived by—a code of honor, rather than an excuse to make rules or control someone else. In fact, Pax seemed to have one heck of a time—a complete inability—to feel less than responsible for someone who needed help.

Which aroused interesting questions, she thought, about who was in Pax's corner. If anyone was now. If anyone ever had been. When he needed help.

He fell into step beside her, at least until she stopped to fumble in the dark cave of her purse. Days before, she'd found a spare house key in a kitchen drawer, but there had to be fifty things in her purse—all of them serious essentials of life. But they sure made finding a tiny key tricky.

When she eventually came up with it, she caught his grin—a patient, tolerant male half grin—that should have exasperated her and instead, sent an immediate blast of awareness hurling through her bloodstream. Pax was damn near irresistible when he relaxed. And when his eyes met hers, she knew he hadn't forgotten those wickedly forbidden kisses from the night before.

She hadn't, either. Although she'd tried to.

"Well, I need to find a way to thank you for helping me this afternoon, and I'm thinking dinner. You'd be risking your life, mind you, and certainly your stomach. But I did have a chance to shop for a few groceries this morning, so I could rustle up something for both of us if your courage level is high."

He chuckled, but his head was shaking before

she finished the invitation. "No, I can't, but thanks."

"Well, damn," she said smoothly, "I should have thought...you probably have a woman friend. I'd really feel badly if I was creating any problems because of your spending time with me..."

"I'm not attached right now and you're not creating a problem. I just have some work I have to do this evening."

Thankfully some men didn't realize when a woman was prying, Kansas thought. So he was alone. And not that she hadn't already guessed that, but forcing herself to behave would have been a lot easier without that confirmation. She'd never have poached on a fellow sister's territory. "Well, if you're busy we can talk another time. I was just hoping you might have some ideas on what I could do next about Case. He mentioned that girl named Serena in his letters. If I could figure out her last name and track her down—"

"I'll do that—see if I can find out her last name. And if I find out anything, I'll give you a call."

"Okay. Well then...I think I'll spend the evening diving into some of the books and papers Case has laying around. Somehow I have to get a better understanding of...*yeeikes!*" Kansas had barely taken a step when she spotted a creature in the shadow of the porch.

Her response time in any emergency had always been clockably fast. She galloped backward, lost a sandal, spun around and determined spit-quick that her rental car was practically a mile away on the other side of the driveway. His Explorer was right there. Faster than she could hyperventilate, she yanked open the passenger side and dived inside.

"What on earth—?"

She motioned with a scarlet-tipped fingernail—from the nice, safe confines of his truck. "I hate to tell you this, but I'm not getting out of here. Possibly not for the rest of the night. Possibly not for the rest of my life. Holy spit, is there *no end* to the horrible, terrifying creatures you have around here? My God, that thing is making me squirm from the inside out. I can't even *look* at him."

Pax swiveled around and immediately noticed the shiny skinned, sharply colored creature sunning in her doorway. He rolled his eyes. "Kansas, it's just a gecko. A two-banded gecko. Nothing more than a lizard, and not in any way poisonous. It won't hurt a soul. In fact, all it does is eat a pile of nasty insects that you probably wouldn't appreciate around anyway. He's a good guy. A friend."

"Pax. Read my lips. I'm not going near that thing, and he and I are *not* going to be friends. Not now, not in fifty years. Not ever."

"Now, come on. You're not that scared. In fact, you'd have a tough time convincing me that you're half the sissy that you let on—"

"I am, too! I am a *total* sissy, a Class A prize-winning coward, a card-carrying gutless wimp. I told you. I need a rescuer. I need a hero. I need a piggyback ride into the house."

"We won't," he said dryly, "need to go that far." He stalked to the porch, bent down and gently shooed the lizard away. The gecko appeared to have no major fear of humans, nor was he in all that much of a hurry to budge. Eventually, though, the prehistoric monster was coaxed into disappearing in the shadows of the bushes. "It's safe to come out now," Pax said wryly.

"So you *say.* What if it comes right back?"

"Kansas, get your fanny out of that truck and quit trying to sell me bologna. I saw how you handled the tarantula the other night."

"I was scared *witless* of that tarantula," she informed him.

"Yeah. I saw." He crooked his finger at her.

Well, shoot. There didn't seem to be a big range of alternative choices, especially considering that she could hardly take root in his truck. After taking a long, cautious look at the bushes, she slowly pulled the door latch and climbed out. "I'm warning you. If that monster steps back up on the porch, I'm gonna shriek loud enough for the mounties to hear me. And I'm talking the mounties in Manitoba."

"Actually I think I should have made you take a closer look at him. If you're going to wander around in the country much, you'd better be able to identify which critters are poisonous and which ones are harmless."

"It'd have taken you and the marines to make me take a closer look at him. And I don't have to worry about which ones are poisonous. I plan on running—fast—from all of them." She reached his side and peered up. "Okay, I admit it, I'm impressed. You handle flaky women well."

"You're not flaky."

True, Kansas thought, but how unnerving to find a man who realized that. Most men defined courage on their own masculine terms. Personally she'd never seen a purpose in conquering her terror of creepy crawly critters. So snakes and spiders gave her the screaming meemies. So what? Kansas had nothing to prove to anyone, and the stuff that was tough to handle in life—pain, grief, loneliness—had no relationship to her behavior around lizards.

Still, she mused, most men freaked out near a little dramatic display of emotion. Not Pax. He was wearing cowboy boots today, she noticed. Sexy cowboy boots. His jeans didn't hug his lanky long legs, but they cuffed his small, flat behind. Evocatively. His expression was evocative, too. Evocatively neutral—no hint of humor, no hint of exasperation, no hint that he was feeling anything at all. He was damn good at that.

At the moment, his hands were on his hips. Waiting, patiently, for her to put the house key into the lock and go inside, so he could take off. "You're sure I can't talk you into dinner?"

"I'm sure."

She pushed the key into the door, then turned back. "I still owe you a thank-you for taking me around this afternoon."

"You're welcome. No sweat."

Men. They understood so little. "I think it's a huge sweat." She firmly corrected him. "I'm imposing on your time. You have absolutely no reason to help me. Maybe I'm worried to death about my brother, but he's *my* brother, no relationship to you and no reason you should feel obligated to give a damn."

"I'm not doing anything that's causing any hardship. When I've got a few free hours, I'm more than willing to help. Not worth making a big deal over."

There now. She caught an expression. Wariness. Even the teensiest glint of alarm in his eyes. She had the fleeting perception that he'd rather take cyanide than a thank-you. Pax was comfortable with trouble, but a little appreciation seemed to knock him for six.

Heaven knew why that perception spurred a sudden impulse. He was so damn tall in those cowboy boots that she had to tilt up on tiptoe...and wrap her palm around his neck to make him bend his head down. Possibly because he had no advance tip what she intended, he never stiffened or pulled back.

She had no advance tip what she intended to do, either...until her lips touched his. It was just a promise of a kiss, more whisper than substance, and over faster than a lady could say "behave yourself." Yet her mouth stayed hovering an inch from his. She felt the sudden tension in his body, saw a swallow shoot down to his Adam's apple, and she understood he was uncomfortable.

She could have been good. She could have rocked back on her heels and left him alone.

Instead she went back for more. One more. Because leaving him alone suddenly struck her as a terrible idea. She'd been standing in that relentless Arizona sunlight, and her mouth was softer, warmer, than a flower petal drenched in the afternoon sun. She just wanted to offer him a drink of that warmth. She just wanted him to taste a little appreciation, and discover it didn't hurt to take it.

Pax's hands moved, faster than a whip, to grip her waist. He was going to push her away, she thought, but that repressive grip almost immediately loosened. His fingers were suddenly kneading her soft flesh, and then not kneading, because his arms swept around her, and he was kissing her back.

Her pulse unraveled like a skein of yarn tumbling down a hillside. Heat clustered low in her belly and feather-fanned all the way to her toes. Her body swayed toward his, into his, as if she had no more power than silver dust to his magnet.

She wasn't trying to resist very hard. He was too alone; Kansas had sensed this before. Alone on the inside. There was a time she'd been just like him—too proud to take help from anyone else, too shamed at the idea of needing anyone. It had taken those long, awful months of being an invalid before she understood that when you lived that way, you shut the door on offering people an opportunity to give.

People had a right to love you. And a need to give as a way of communicating caring.

It was damn selfish to not let them.

And damn lonely.

It was that brand of loneliness she sensed in him. His kisses were more rough than skilled, and his hands, roving her back, were more wild than deliberate. Pax was no invalid. Not as she'd been once. But he didn't seem to know that revealing a little need wasn't going to hurt him. Expressing need was no weakness. It was just human.

And maybe she kept giving, kept offering him more, because his response was so delicious. Rough and real. Reaching something rough and real inside her. Longings. Longings so naked and vulnerable that they had no name. Desire so sudden and fierce that she just wanted to ride it, like a roller coaster, because excitement this wondrous never happened to her. Except with him. The damn man had done it to her last night, too. She didn't know how. And she didn't know why it had to be Pax. She just knew that there wasn't a man alive who'd ever made her feel... dangerous. Ever. Before him.

His hands cupped her fanny, squeezed her tight against him, making her shiver from the inside out, making her intimately aware of what he was packing in those jeans. It was time to cool this down, she thought, time to get smart. Yet she couldn't seem to stir up any interest in getting smart. His hands were on the road again. Her pulse accelerated like a hot-rod engine, and another hot shiver sluiced down her spine when his hand traveled around to the front of her dress.

His palm burned through the cotton knit fabric, bunching the thin material, claiming the soft skin of her abdomen in an exploring caress before climbing up to her ribs. By the time his thumb brushed the underwire base of her bra, she'd quit breathing.

He hadn't. He was breathing hard and hoarse, breathing into her, breathing into a kiss that did an extraordinary job of turning her heartbeat to butter...but she knew where that thumb of his was. She knew exactly. Her breasts were already taut, already sensitive and aching and chafing at the confinement of the underwire torture device, but the bra thankfully had a front clasp. His thumb was a half inch from it. His hand didn't have to move far, and her heart was beating like a crazy clock, anticipating, expecting, waiting unbearably for his fingers to flip that latch and cover her, knowing as sure as she was born that intimacy was coming.

"Dammit, Kansas."

His fingers connected, all right. In the form of knuckles right under her chin. He'd cut off that kiss with the harshness of a knife slice, but her face was still tilted to his. She could see his expression. He was not a happy camper.

"I thought you were so damn terrified of lizards."

"Hmm?" His voice was rusty and low, his eyes darker than liquid smoke. Haunted smoke. She'd been so busy coping with her world spinning that it took a second to realize she'd spun his world, too. Pax so fiercely valued invulnerability. She couldn't stop looking at that deep, dark vulnerability in his eyes.

"What happened to all that shrieking terror about the lizards? You haven't even looked down. For all you know, that little gecko could be sitting on your foot right now—and you wouldn't give a holy damn."

"Hmm?" So, she mused, it was damns this time instead of hells. At least he wasn't wasting his breath apologizing. If Kansas were inclined to be wildly optimistic, she just might call that making headway.

"Stop saying hmm. And stop looking at me like that. You're the most incomprehensible woman—the things you're supposed to be afraid of, you're not. The things that aren't worth a second thought give you the shrieks. Dammit, Kansas. You *have* to know what real danger is."

"You think I should be afraid of you?"

"I think you should be afraid of inviting something you don't want to happen."

"Okay," she murmured, "I will be very careful from now on *not* to invite anything I don't want to happen."

His brow bunched in a frown that was thicker than thunderclouds. She'd certainly tried to respond to his concern, but the nature of her answer didn't seem to please him worth spit.

"Kansas, I'm serious," he warned her.

"So," she promised, "am I."

Five

The instant his truck popped into the driveway, Kansas pelted out of the house and hustled for the door. ''So you found Serena? My brother's girlfriend?''

''I haven't met her, Kansas. All I found out was that her last name is Madieros and that she works in Tombstone. It's about a twenty-minute drive from here—''

He'd told her some of this in a telephone call before coming over, but Kansas had barely slept the night before and was fuzzy from a nap when he called. For sure, she hadn't caught the name of the town where they were going. "Tombstone? We're really going to Tombstone? You mean the town too tough to die? Wyatt Earp and the OK Corral and Boot Hill and all that?"

"Yeah, I mean that tourist trap," Pax said dryly. "And I don't know if it's such a great idea to try to connect with her there. If she's working, she could be too busy to talk. But now was the time I had a few hours free, so if you wanted to at least get a look at her—"

"I do," Kansas assured him. In the few seconds it took her to belt in, she felt his gaze sliding over her, lingering on her bare legs and the simple white shorts and T-shirt. Momentarily he looked startled, but he didn't say a word, just turned his attention to backing out of the driveway.

It was eighty-five lung-parching, sun-baking degrees even this early in the afternoon. Considering this godforsaken climate, Pax was lucky she hadn't shown up naked, and if he was surprised to see her in plain old ordinary clothes instead her usual flamboyant attire...well better for her. If a helpless city slicker image made Pax more willing to help with her brother, she'd have worn gold lame cut to the navel. But he had already volunteered his help. And by Kansas's value system, there was a time when a woman could justifiably resort to fakery, and a time when a woman needed to come clean.

He'd scared her last night. Scared her enough so that she'd been pacing the floors in the wee hours of the morning, unable to sleep, unable to even lay her head down.

The picture kept flashing in front of her mind from the evening before. Pax, warning her not to invite trouble. Pax, with his eyes darker than moonbeams, his face carved with taut lines of control, and an innocuously sunlit driveway so charged with electricity that Kansas figured they were lucky it didn't smoke.

All night, she'd imagined making love with him. All night, she'd reminded herself that every experience she'd had with overprotective men was a telling omen. Pax was protective. She knew ahead that meant a relationship had terrible odds of working. She knew ahead that it was an ominously bad idea to fall in love with him.

Yet she seemed to be falling fast, hard and helplessly. And it was the strangest thing. Somehow she couldn't shake the crazy, outlandish notion that for the first time, she'd found a man who needed her instead of the other way around. For the first time, she'd found a man who needed protecting—and a woman's brand and breed of strength—if he just didn't shut the door before she could show him what that meant.

He'd shut that door awfully tight last night, though. And if she sensed how deeply he could matter to her, she also sensed that he could be hurt. Chemistry had blown up between them with a bludgeoning fast speed, though. And of all the times to be considering taking emotional risks, this one just about couldn't be worse.

God knew, she had other mountainously serious problems on her mind. "Pax..." She leaned her head back against the headrest. "I waded into several of those books Case had laying around. One was about the Aztecs and their religion. Apparently the Aztecs—at least by legend—used two drugs, datura and peyote, to produce visions as part of certain religious rituals. Datura. Isn't that the plant you said Case was growing in the living room?"

"It isn't the common term for that plant today, but yeah, it looked like it."

"And I saw your expression when you noticed that plant. You think my brother was growing it to use as a drug, don't you?"

"I never said that, Kansas."

"Well, it isn't true. Case *never* played around with either drugs or alcohol. Ever. The kind of trouble he got into was pure bad judgment and mischief, but he steered clear of the drug crowd and hated that whole scene. Adamantly. He always said life was all he needed to get high on.''

''People can change,'' Pax said quietly. ''Hadn't it been some long months since you'd seen him?''

''It doesn't matter. He didn't change, not in that direction. I *know* him. Maybe there was some other reason why he was growing that plant. Maybe he thought it was something else.''

''Maybe.''

''Quit looking at me like you think I need a bullet from a reality gun. I'm *not* naive.''

''Yes, ma'am.''

''And don't call me ma'am.''

Pax cleared his throat. ''By any chance, are we a little touchy today?''

Touchy didn't begin to cut it. When Kansas was short on sleep, she was crabbier than a porcupine, and it didn't help that she was restless and edgy and increasingly scared for her brother. ''I read some other things, too. I found another book laying around about some kind of old, Native American religion. The basic beliefs were about worshiping the earth and natural things. Respect for animals and nature. That sounded very much like something that would interest my brother, but I'm telling you, there was nothing weird or wild about it. Nothing! Except..."

"Except what?"

"Except that there was quite a focus on meditation and psychic visions." She rushed on swiftly and stubbornly. "I happen to believe in psychic phenomenon. I don't think there's any question that some people have special perceptions. They can see things ahead, or feel things about other people. I know there are some quacks and fakes out there, but that doesn't take away from the real people who have some real gifts."

"Kansas?"

"What?"

"I keep having the feeling that you're expecting me to attack your brother. Honey, if I wanted my throat cut, I'd hit a redneck bar at two in the morning. I have absolutely no death wish. I got nicknamed Pax because of being a peace lover."

He'd called her honey, she noticed. And the endearment settled in her stomach like hopelessly warm fuzz. "Are you...um...tactfully trying to suggest that I can get a wee bit defensive about my brother?"

"I think you'd charge into a lion den for your brother and not think twice. But as it happens, I'm not a lion. And on the subject of psychic phenomenon, I wasn't about to disagree."

"You weren't?"

"No. I don't know that I'm fond of that word 'psychic,' but many of the Native American religions sought visions through fasting and meditation. Mysticism may have been part of those beliefs, but basically you're just talking about people seeking meaning and spiritual insights. I think they were right—that we could all pick up self-perception if we opened our minds. We're part of our earth, part of our planet, and it wouldn't hurt any of us to meditate some on how we fit into the whole."

Kansas swiveled in the seat, swinging a leg under her, her gaze riveted on Pax's face. "You talked with my brother about this, didn't you?"

"More than once," Pax admitted. "But only to a point. I knew he'd picked up a fascination for some of those ideas. Nothing wrong with that, that I saw. I think everyone has a spiritual side—but I also think it's a matter of the heart. I don't mess with anyone's personal beliefs of the heart."

"Pax? Dammit, what are you *not* telling me?"

His gaze honed on her face for a few short seconds before returning to the road. "I think people are vulnerable about their personal beliefs, Kansas. Especially young people, who are just exploring their feelings about meaning and life and all that other good nonsense. And in the wrong hands, even the most innocent idea can be reinterpreted, taken too far."

"Geezle beezle, would you quit beating around the bush? Just tell me straight what you think my brother was involved in. You're not talking about a Koresh kind of scene, are you? Some commune or cult where the kids have been brainwashed?"

"Now take it easy. I don't know anything for sure—I've told you before—but I never heard one word about a ringleader or anything organized at that serious a level. All I'm aware of was a group of kids who started going off in the hills to meditate together, who'd become real involved in this private religion of theirs. In the beginning, no one thought anything of it. But there started to be some talk about witches and 'cleansing rituals'—which was a small part of those old beliefs back when. And some of those kids dropped out, way out. But just because your brother was reading and interested is absolutely no proof that Case was directly involved," Pax repeated, and then said, "We're here."

Kansas jerked her head toward the window for her first view of Tombstone. Pax was challenged to find a parking space on even the side streets. Tourists were as packed on the road as the sidewalks. Except for the tourists, the town could have been a step back to a hundred years ago.

Cowboys in chaps and Stetsons and dusty boots strolled the sidewalks—wearing six-shooters—and some duded up in buckskin and fringe. A few of the women wore long calico dresses, while others were gussied up with face paint and low-cut satin gowns with miles of tucks and flounces. Bawdy music spilled from a building marked the Bird Cage Theater. Signs pointed to the OK Corral. Low-slung, wooden buildings were covered with dust, and the shuttered doors swung open from the Crystal Palace saloon.

It was wonderful. It was charming and delightful and fascinating, how the town had chosen to recreate history and make it so real. But Kansas rubbed the back of her neck, feeling as disoriented as a hummingbird suddenly thrown into a swimming pool. Her mind just wasn't on this.

Hot day or not, her skin felt chilled and her nerves felt shaky. Witches. Case was involved in some kind of witch cult. All along, she'd intuited that he was in some kind of danger, but she'd been hand wringing that he was lost or had broken his leg or something like that. In a thousand years, she'd never envisioned that her happy-go-lucky brother could fall off this type of deep end.

Abruptly she became aware that Pax was standing there, patiently holding the passenger door open for her. "I have to find him," she said fiercely. "If he's involved in anything like a cult, I have to find him and get him out."

"No purpose in borrowing trouble, red. There isn't one damn thing you know for sure—and neither do I. Not at this point."

"I don't care. I have to *do* something! Now!"

"We *are* doing something. We're going to get a look at the girl Case was involved with."

Serena. Kansas scooched out of the truck faster than a jet-propelled rocket the instant she remembered the girl.

If Pax had a choice, he'd never have mentioned anything about witches or cult worship to Kansas. It wasn't a question of hiding information from her. She had a right to know about her brother. But until facts had surfaced, he saw no reason to worry her with wild suppositions that could prove unfounded. Red tended to react so emotionally that he was afraid she'd go off half-cocked and do God-knows-what.

Unfortunately all the clues surfacing about her brother seemed to be aimed in same direction. Pax had tried to soften the edges and temper her reaction with common sense. As he should have guessed, that effort was like throwing water down a drain.

Once he told Kansas their destination—the OK Corral—she galloped down the sidewalk at a pace designed to mow down everyone else. She barreled into the tourist office faster than a gunman with a date for a shoot-out at high noon.

Then, thankfully, she slowed down and took a breath.

They both identified Serena Madieros from the girl's name tag. She was one of the three employees manning the ticket counter for the next show—which was imminent, judging from the packed crowd. Clearly there would be no chance to catch a word with the girl until that was done, but the waiting gave him and Kansas a chance to look her over.

Pax judged Serena's age in the late teens. Her long raven hair was coiled in an old-fashioned style, suited to the period costume she was wearing—a calico dress with some frilly lace around the neck. Pax saw the flashing black eyes. The oval face with no makeup or artifice. The slim hands, with the nails cut short and no nail paint.

"Why, she's a darling," Kansas murmured.

Since Kansas—typically—had stopped dead in the thick of traffic, he steered her to a corner out of harm's way. "We have a saying in the Southwest. *Buenas son mis vecinas, perio me faltan tres gallinas.* My neighbors are nice, but I'm still missing three chickens.''

''Chickens?''

''If you want a more literal translation—maybe it's not always wise to judge a person by their looks. Even if they look nice.''

Kansas chuckled, clearly amused. ''I'm beginning to fall in love with some of your sayings around here.''

Pax was beginning to fall in love—in a figurative sense, of course—with watching her operate. As soon as the crowd thinned out, Kansas ordered him to stay put while she approached the girl alone. Her reasoning was that Serena might open up more easily in a one-on-one conversation with another woman.

Pax had no argument with that idea, but he thought Kansas had a lot of future on the stage—or as a politician. She'd put on quite a dog-and-pony show for the man in the bookstore—thrusting her chest out, dampening her lips, teasing poor George so mercilessly that he blurted out an answer to anything she asked.

There was none of that nonsense with Serena. It was other nonsense. The shy, reserved woman who walked up to the counter had little in common with Kansas. Her hands were clasped modestly together, her shoulders rounded, and her expression appealingly apologetic as she phrased her first question to Serena.

Pax recognized it was her wimp routine, just in another form. But it was still like trying to understand the intricacies of an alien from another planet. She was unquestionably shook up about her brother. When he was shook up about something, he shut down and got tough. He approached any difficult problem coming from strength—the instinct to protect himself so automatic that he never had to think about it.

Kansas approached a problem as if she was wearing a neon sign: This Is Where I'm Vulnerable. The act with George had never been entirely a lie, and this stage play with Serena had the same elements of truth—Kansas was dealing the other person a hand of cards faceup, revealing exactly where she could be hurt.

She kissed the same way.

Pax was trying damn hard to forget how she kissed—but the limitless ways that redhead set herself up to be crushed still had a disastrous effect on his blood pressure. Until he met Kansas, he'd barely been aware he even *had* blood pressure.

Her encounter with Serena only lasted twenty minutes. More Wyatt Earp and gunfight fans started wandering in; Serena had a job to do, and Kansas stepped away and flew back to his side.

There was none of that endearing shy action for him, he noticed. Her eyes were ablaze with frustration. "She's a sweetie and a darling, but she hasn't seen Case in two weeks herself. She lives with her parents, works on their ranch weekends and here during the week. Three younger sisters. When she gets enough money together, she wants to take some college courses, probably in accounting—"

He pushed open the door. "You got her entire life history in less than twenty minutes?"

"A woman knows how to talk to another woman. You fellas just wouldn't understand." She ducked under his arm and zoomed outside. If they were headed to the truck at the same pace her mind was racing, it was going to be one fast jog. "She's a real serious girl. Good kid. She met my brother at some barn dance thing. She liked him from the start—they'd been seeing quite a bit of each other—but she was pretty wary in the beginning, because he didn't have a job, didn't seem to be serious about his future—"

From nowhere she suddenly stumbled. Instinctively Pax hooked an arm around her shoulder so she couldn't fall. As if his hormones had been laying in ambush for the first excuse to touch her, fire stoked and stroked through his veins. Memories of last night rushed through his mind—unwanted—and especially not now. In that flash of a second before she caught her balance, he saw her wince, saw her face turn stark white with pain. ''Are you okay? What happened?''

Her eyes averted from his faster than a skittery filly, and she took off again—leaving his arm hanging in midair. ''Serena said he was changing. She said they spent hours talking, just talking—no matter what her parents believed they were doing. She thought Case was really changing his life around. He'd gotten a real job, was serious about keeping it—''

''Kansas, stop trying to walk so fast. What's wrong with your knee?''

''Nothing. I just tripped because I'm a clumsy klutz...she went on and on about my brother, about the kinds of things they talked about, dreams, ideals they both believed in, spiritual things, communing with nature—''

''What's wrong with your knee?'' Pax repeated.

''She said everyone else thought he was a ne'er-do-well who was never going to take anything seriously, but it wasn't true. He'd just never taken the time to think about goals before, and she'd been real hurt when he stopped calling two weeks ago—thought he'd dropped her. She's not part of any witch nonsense, Pax. Or any religious cult, either. She's just a girl, a nice girl—''

''Just so we're real clear on this, you are *not* going to continue walking on a limp like that. Either you start talking fast about what kind of injury you're dealing with, or you're gonna get picked up and carried the rest of the way to the truck.''

''Oh, for pete's sake,'' Kansas said crossly. She stopped dead with her hands on her hips.

For a quarter, Pax bet, she'd box his ears—even if she had to reach up a half foot to do it. Maybe he should have guessed from that flame and fiery tumble of red hair that Kansas had a flash temper. No way, no how, was the lady going to take a threat lying down—no matter how kindly that threat was intended. Her lips were parted, and he braced, expecting to hear a lecture designed to put him in his place—which was conceivably lower than a worm hole at that moment.

But then she abruptly closed her mouth. Her forehead creased in a considering frown, and her eyes searched his intently. Pax had no clue what was suddenly so important to her, or what she was trying to make up her mind about. But in the turnaround of a minute, she apparently forgot about being ticked off with him.

"If you want to hear it, I'll tell you the story about how I got this limp—but right now I'm dying of thirst," she said swiftly. "How about if we find someplace where we can sit down and buy a pop?"

The Crystal Palace was open for business. Dusty sunlight fell on the long polished bar and plank wooden floor. Pax could easily picture cowboys playing poker while ladies of ill repute served drinks in days of yore, but days of yore couldn't have interested him less right then.

He steered Kansas to a table under the window, as far away from the noise as possible, then hustled to the bar. By the time he brought back two sweating mugs of old-fashioned root beer, he saw Kansas was not only sitting down, but no longer trying to hide how badly her right leg was hurting her. She'd perched her ankle on the leg of a chair, and was using both hands to massage her right knee cap.

She quit that, though, as soon as she spotted the mugs of root beer. "I take back every terrible thing I ever said about you. You're my hero for life. I'm so thirsty I could die."

He ignored the dramatic avowal—the damn woman was always making dramatic avowals—

and he waited patiently until she'd swallowed a long, greedy throatful of the root beer. ''Taste good?''

''Like nectar and heaven.''

''Good. That's good.'' Because her thirst was obviously sincere, he waited until she gulped down another fizzy slug. But that was about as long as he could stand waiting. ''So tell me what happened to your leg.''

''I will...but if it's all right, I'd like to ask you something first.'' She grabbed a napkin to wrap around her sweating glass. ''From the first time I met you, you struck me as being a loner. Not that you aren't wonderful with people—the whole town seems to know you. But on the inside, you seem to be an independent, self-reliant kind of person...I'd guess it would really bother you if you were stuck depending on others?''

''Kansas, what the Sam Hill does my being a loner have anything to do with your leg?'' he asked impatiently.

She took another sip of root beer. ''I didn't mean to pry. You certainly don't have to answer that question if you don't want to.''

Fathoming Kansas's mind was like trying to tiptoe through quicksand, but Pax figured he wasn't going to get anywhere unless he catered to her.

"No reason not to answer you. My background's no secret. Yeah, I've been an independent cuss from the get-go, came by that attitude pretty naturally. My mom died young, and my dad took off while I was still in high school—I was about seventeen, and he left me without a penny in the till or a can in the larder." Pax shrugged. "It wasn't as rough as it sounds. I learned how to take care of myself, and did just fine. And yeah, I like people and I've made good friends, but when push comes down to shove, I depend on myself, no one else. Does that answer your question?"

"Oh, yes," she said softly.

Pax didn't like the way she was looking at him, as if that convoluted feminine mind were clicking puzzle pieces into place that only she could see. It made him feel uneasy. It made him feel...nervous. Which was ridiculous. Pax knew damn well he didn't have a nervous bone in his entire body. "Kansas, what possible relationship could there be between my background and your limp?"

"Everything," she said simply. "It shows how differently we learned to relate to people, because of the different experiences we had. I never had a chance to learn self-reliance—nor did I have any choice about depending on other people.''

''No choice?''

''I was in a car accident when I was fourteen. Broke some ribs, my right knee, did a little pretzel routine on my spine,'' she said lightly and guzzled another sip of root beer. ''There was some question whether I'd walk again. Took almost a year before I could—even a few steps. For a real long time, I was stuck being a pain-in-the-behind invalid. I just had no way to do anything for myself.''

Pax expected to hear about an accident or injury, but nothing this bad. The waitresses sashaying around, the tourists scrabbling for tables, the bartender's booming laugh all faded to another place. All he saw was Kansas's eyes, bluer and clearer than the sky. He thought of that irrepressible and indomitable spirit cooped up in a hospital bed, and a fist of emotion squeezed around his heart. ''I'm sorry, red,'' he said awkwardly. ''That's real rough. I didn't know. I had a feeling there was something in your background, because every time you talked about your brother—''

''Yeah. I know you think I'm blind-loyal to Case, but that's the reason—because once upon a time, he gave me that same kind of blind loyalty. He was just a little squirt then, but he spent hours with me, cheering me on every time I wanted to give up. I'm not deserting him now, Pax. He was just a snot-nosed, freckled kid, but he was the one who taught me that's what love is—being there when someone needs you. However..."

He watched her cross her arms on the table, and hunch forward as if she wanted to be sure she had his attention. She had his attention. The wayward strand of hair curling at her throat, the butter-soft mouth, the spray of freckles on the bridge of her nose, those eyes so rich and deep with emotion that a man could drown in them. Oh, yeah. She had his attention. "However?" he echoed vaguely.

"However...I wanted you to know I'd been honest with you. I told you I was a wimp and a weakling, and that was always true. Basically I couldn't be healthier now, but physically—I'll never be as strong as an Amazon. I'm short on stamina, and if I do something stupid, my right knee can give out on me faster than spit."

Essentially, Pax thought, she was telling him that she'd always, honestly, needed his help. Her wuss routine might have been occasionally put-on, but taking off cross country to find her brother alone was no simple task for her.

He had a sudden doomed feeling, like an avalanche was about to spill on his head. He already had honed masculine instincts to warn him away from certain kinds of trouble. Any woman who swept the rug out from under his self-control was on that list. A woman who was disastrously his opposite in life-styles, who did nothing he could comprehend, who galloped toward problems with no logic or common sense, who was diametrically different from any female he'd been attracted to—all those things were on his list. A grown man simply knew better than to ask for heartache.

But if he'd felt protective before, her whole story about that accident made him feel blindsided by the power of protective feelings for her now.

There was no way he could desert her.

Six

Two days later Kansas pulled into Pax's driveway. As she climbed from the rental car, the contrast between the Civic's exuberant air-conditioning to the sudden blast of heat stole her breath. Even this early in the day, the desert sun could bake an icicle before it had a chance to melt. Still, her gaze riveted on the look of Pax's place. It was the first time she'd seen it.

Driving here had been an impulse. She had news she wanted to share with him, but telephoning had only connected her with his answering machine and a message about his being in surgery all morning. From that she'd concluded that he was here, for sure, and although she felt guilty for intruding on his workday, she only wanted a few seconds of his time.

As Kansas slowly looked around, she forgot the blistering heat and mentally tossed that guilt in a trash heap.

Pax, she mused, badly needed someone to intrude in his life, because it was increasingly clear that no one else had.

He'd never mentioned that his vet office was connected to his home. The white adobe house sprawled, ranch style, with a orange-tiled roof that glinted in the sun. Although the property was located way out of town, Pax had further secluded the grounds by bordering the place with a white stone privacy wall. She could see a barn-type building in back with a fenced-in area that she assumed was for animals. The vet sign in the yard was sun bleached and faded. A couple of century plants and cacti comprised the whole landscaping, and they looked scrubby. The house was nice—beyond nice—but the dusty windows and lack of curtains indicated that no woman had been around long enough to fuss with the place.

Three cats shot from nowhere and swarmed around her legs as she reached the front door. The trio could have competed in a homeliness contest. The striped tiger was missing an ear; the tortoiseshell had a clipped tail; and a black-and-white spotted waif had a naked side stripped of fur. Kansas instinctively crouched down to pet the attention-beggars, and was immediately caught in a jealous meow fest over who got stroked first.

Eventually—it took some time—she stood up and knocked on the door. No answer. She poked her head in. "Pax?"

His voice came from some room down a hallway to the right. "I'm back here in the surgery. It'll be a few minutes. Kansas, is that you?"

"Yeah, it's me."

"Are you okay? Is something wrong?"

"I'm fine and nothing's wrong. I just had something I needed to tell you."

"Well, I'll be out as soon as I can. There's coffee in the kitchen, if you can find yourself a mug."

She didn't want coffee, but she definitely didn't mind a few minutes alone to roam around. Another cat—even more beat-up than the ones outside—blinked at her from the depths of an old easy chair. Pax's office was apparently his living room. A desk and file cabinets took up a third of the space. A computer, fax and answering machine made his setup self-sufficient—no reason for a receptionist—but the splashes of high-tech equipment jarred with the rest of his decor.

Indian molas hung from the walls, framing an old fashioned kiva fireplace in the corner. Barrister-style bookshelves were sardine-packed with medical texts. The rust-colored couch was long enough for Lincoln to sleep on, but could have used recovering a decade ago. The whole room looked as dusty as the sleepy cat.

A rounded doorway led into a virgin white kitchen. In a glance she took in the table heaped with mail and magazines and work—no space for a plate, much less food. The counters and sink were spit-shine clean, but there wasn't a curtain or rug, no feminine touch to soften the austerity. Sun blazed hot through the windows. A chambray shirt hung abandoned on a chair.

Sliding glass doors opened onto a shaded patio, but Kansas didn't waste time looking outside. Who knew how long Pax would be occupied? If she only had a few minutes to seriously snoop and pry, the inside had to be the best source of secrets.

Unconsciously tiptoeing, she found a mudroom with jackets and outdoor gear, and across from that, she poked her head into the bathroom for a quick study. Dark green towels hung neatly, but the walls were an unadorned white. Around the sink counter were a straight razor, no nonsense soap and shaving cream—no luxury items for Pax.

At the end of that hall was his bedroom. It should have been a sybaritic paradise. The room was long enough to skate in, with a skylight and slanted ceiling and the space for all kinds of interesting activities. Instead there was a plain double bed, no headboard, the white sheets rumpled and unmade, no rug, no warmth, no trace that a woman had ever slept here.

Kansas leaned against the doorjamb, catching the loneliness implicit in that empty rumpled bed, sensing the barren solitude in every corner of the house she'd seen so far.

Two days before in Tombstone, she'd hesitated hard before confessing her invalid childhood. Men invariably responded with pity and sympathy and all that protective nonsense that drove her bananas, but it was different with Pax. Sharing a personal secret led him to share his. She had no way to know that he'd been deserted and abandoned by his father, left to fend for himself, but suddenly it was much easier to understand why Pax stiffened up when people got close.

She wondered if he'd ever allowed a woman to spoil or pamper him or if any woman had stayed long enough to do so. She wondered if he'd even experienced the simple luxury of being cared for—and suspected not. Once he revealed his background, Kansas understood that he equated depending on other people with root canals, taxes, brussels sprouts. Alone was easier. Alone was safer.

Alone was damn stupid.

He needed a lover, she thought fiercely, and he needed one badly. Not just any old lover, but a woman who'd knock him three sides of Sunday, who understood the difference between physical and emotional strength, who could give him an unforgettable lesson that expressing need and risking hurt were not an automatic equation. And since a woman who dared try pampering Pax would likely get her head bitten off, she'd better be tough up-front.

Kansas could define this potential lover of Pax's in painstaking detail.

She just wasn't sure if she had the guts, arrogance, or terrifying nerve to apply for the job.

"Hey...if you were about to look in my drawers, don't let me stop you."

Lord, he'd startled her! With her heart in her throat, Kansas spun around. "I would *never* do such a thing..." Since her own mother wouldn't buy such a blatant lie, she quickly amended that.

''At least when there was any risk of being caught.''

To her relief, Pax chuckled at her honesty. ''Now why am I not convinced that fear of being caught would inhibit you one iota?''

''Hey, I have the usual bucket load of inhibitions. It's just that curiosity is a terribly powerful motivator.'' Maybe it was her put-on prim tone that made him chuckle again, but he really didn't seem too irritated to find her snooping. Kansas thought she shouldn't have been surprised. Pax often exhibited endless tolerance with other people's flaws. It was his own he had no patience with.

Neither seemed inclined to dwell on what she was doing in his bedroom.

She watched him wiping his hands on a towel—he must have come from his surgery, although instead of a lab coat, he was wearing a navy T-shirt tucked into faded jeans. His feet were in sandals, his raven hair yanked back in a leather thong. Although his eyes looked bruised-tired, there was no tiredness in the way he looked her over.

His gaze skimmed the bumps and curves in her short black skimp, skimmed her choice of moon and star earrings and equally whimsical bracelet, but he neither lingered on her attire nor her figure. She felt his eyes on her face like honey clinging to toast—he hadn't forgotten kissing her. He hadn't forgotten touching her.

"So...who was the patient you were treating this morning?" It wasn't news for her, that sling of heat and curling-toes awareness of him. But the raw desire in his eyes was big news. She had the pulse-pounding feeling that she wasn't the only one considering auditioning a lover in his bed, but that naked emotion in his face disappeared in a blink. Pax suddenly quit wiping his hands on that towel, and his expression switched to neutral faster than a race-car driver could downshift.

"My patient was a German shepherd whose days of seducing the gals in the neighborhood are now over. He'll be sleeping off the anesthetic for a while—and I don't know what you wanted to tell me, but I'm pretty desperate for coffee. I've been playing in the surgery since sunup."

Pax had barely turned around to head for the kitchen before the tortoiseshell cat showed up to weave around his ankles; the fight victim from the living room found him right after that. "I hate cats," he called over his shoulder.

"I can see that."

"These cats aren't mine. None of 'em are mine. And in the six years I've lived here, there hasn't been one good-looking cat who dropped in—it's always the mangy, ugly, godforsaken-looking ones that no one in their right minds would ever adopt. I fix 'em. Assuming they aren't pregnant when they arrive—which most of them are. As far as I can tell, there *are* no male cats. Only pregnant female ones."

"What an interesting scientific viewpoint for a vet to have," Kansas said wryly. "You think they get that way by immaculate conception?"

"I wouldn't put it past them. God knows they're contrary in every other way. If I were *going* to have a pet—which I'm gone way too much to have time for—it'd be a dog. It would never be a cat."

"Ah." Once in the kitchen, she watched Mr. Anticat Tough-Guy refill a giant size food dish with cat food—before pouring the coffee for himself that he was so desperate for. Somewhere there had to be a pet door, because the rest of the feline herd showed up in a swarm. Since he was busy, she opened cupboards to find a mug for him. The coffeemaker was already half full—although the brew looked blacker than pitch. "You take sugar? Cream?"

"No."

"Of course not," she murmured. He'd take his

coffee as minimalist as his life-style. No sweetness, no softness, no luxuries.

"What does that 'of course not' mean?"

"Nothing. Just talking to myself—where do you want this?"

"Out on the patio."

In the air. With the bugs and heat. She sighed. At least it was only blistering and not die-of-misery hot yet, and the patio was shaded. Carrying his mug, she pushed open the sliding glass doors. Outside, a wrought-iron lounger and chairs clustered around a glass table. She noticed a dozen bird feeders in the yard, all shapes and sizes.

Pax followed her, leaving the door open. A terrorizing way to let tarantulas and scorpions in, she thought, but it was his house. No matter how much she wanted to pry further around his house, his life—and him—Kansas was regretfully aware that she had not been invited. And for a few minutes, she'd almost forgotten the serious reason she'd stopped by.

"Pax," she said, "I think I know where my brother is."

Pax heard the excitement in her voice, and felt a prompt heavy thud in his stomach. For two days his life had been calm, normal, peaceful.

He'd almost forgotten what she did to him. Likely Kansas would object to being handcuffed to a chair, but so far every time she'd been restless and excited—about anything—she somehow managed to turn his entire reasonable world into a pile of Pick Up Sticks. "Okay, so where do you think Case is?"

"In the Coronado Forest. I brought a map—" She'd barely sat down before she was bouncing up again. She hustled to the wrought-iron patio table to grab her shoulder bag.

"Wait. I already know where the Coronado Forest is. First just tell me why you think he's there."

"Because I went to see a woman this morning. I happened to notice the address for this psychic healer in the telephone book—"

"Aw hell, Kansas." He rolled his eyes.

"Now, don't get your liver in an uproar. I didn't look her up to check out her healing talents...although, heavens, I'd have loved to see her 'laying on some hands.' But not today. I just went to see her because I hoped her interest in mysticism and psychic phenomenon might give me some kind of lead to my brother. And it did. She started talking about all kinds of sacred Indian grounds in the area. Historical holy places, like where native people traditionally went to meditate or just gather to share their beliefs, and she specifically mentioned this spot called *'Valle de Oro'* in the Coronado. Wouldn't that make sense to you? That kids pursuing some kind of ritualistic religion or cult thing would be drawn to a place like that?''

''Yeah, it makes sense. And yeah, that's not the first time that area crossed my mind as a location for where those kids are setting up camp.''

She sank in a chair and stared at him. ''You already knew? And you didn't tell me?''

Pax washed a hand over his face. There was always a problem with talking to Kansas. It was impossible to maintain a logical thought train when she responded to everything emotionally. She expressed hurt over nothing he could imagine would hurt her; she argued and teased and spilled things about herself as if they'd known each other for years. She talked as if...as if she felt *close* to him, as if she *knew* him, and damnation, it was an unfair way to rattle a man. ''Kansas, what exactly do you think you can do with that information?''

''Find my brother. Go get him.''

''Honey, there are twelve mountain ranges in the Coronado, covering almost two million acres.''

"I realize it's a big area, but *all* those acres aren't sacred ground—"

"True. But you're still talking about finding a needle in a haystack, because places like that aren't listed on any map. The Native people never advertised the location of those so-called holy places for the obvious reason. They didn't want outsiders to find them. And there are parts of the Coronado that are wilder than anything you can imagine. Places that never have seen a road. Places you can't even travel by horseback, and places where you sure as hell can't take an air-conditioned car—even if you knew exactly where you were going and what you were looking for."

"I don't care."

"No? Are you ready to carry a fifty-pound backpack in the desert? Do you know anything about the terrain? Do you have any idea how to protect yourself against dehydration? What are you gonna do if you run across a rattlesnake?"

"If I come within a mile of a rattlesnake, you can have a written guarantee—I'll scream bloody murder. But somehow I don't seem to be making myself clear. I don't give a holy spit about snakes or dehydration. I'll do whatever I have to do. I'm going to find my brother, Pax. If you don't want to help me—"

Damn, but she was bouncing out of that chair faster than a speeding bullet. Dynamite had to be less volatile. "I never said that. Would you just sit down and calm down and let me think for two seconds?" Pax rubbed a hand over his jaw. "You haven't been to where Case worked yet—there hasn't been time—and maybe his boss or the other employees know something. More to the point, if you come across some concrete information, the place to go back to is the sheriff."

"I'm more than willing to check out where Case worked. And even if the sheriff didn't listen to me the first time, I'll be glad to try him again. But if I find out where this cult is located, I'm going there. With or without help. No matter what anyone says."

"Red, you're assuming trouble that may not exist. Your brother could still show up any day, flat broke and tanned from a helluva wild vacation."

"Yeah, I keep telling myself that, too." All the stuffing and starch went out of her shoulders. When she met his gaze, her naked heart was right in her eyes. "But I don't believe it. I'm scared, Pax. And getting more scared all the time. The longer he's missing, the more I'm positive that he's in real trouble. Trouble he can't get out of on his own."

Pax thought the same thing. There was too much talk in town about this cult. Talk of witches and drugs and a camping hideout buried deep in the hills. It always sounded too wild to believe, and being a peace lover and a man who never minded other people's business, he paid no attention.

Before, though, he had no reason to worry or care whether the gossip possibly had a base of truth. *"Cuando el rio suena, agua lleva,"* he murmured.

"Another one of your Southwestern sayings?"

"Yeah. When the river makes noise, it's carrying water. Loosely translated, it means that most rumors have some foundation." Pax lurched to his feet. Maybe Kansas's restlessness was contagious. He'd never had a problem sitting still before.

He'd never had a problem getting a woman off his mind before, either—not if a woman was as unlike him as night and day. He refused to believe that Kansas was a threat to his heart, but she was sure as hell a threat to his sanity—and damned if he knew what to do about her.

If push came down to shove, he could go off himself to find Case. Where others saw the desert as bleak and hostile, he'd always seen the beauty, always related at some simpatico level with the wild and lonely spirit of the country. Over the years, he'd come to know the desert like the back of his hand. He'd rescued more than one tourist who blithely misunderstood how dangerous this country could be.

But Kansas had to be kept out of any such rescue mission, and so far Pax hadn't noticed one thing that the lady kept her nose out of. She dove headfirst and think last into everything—but her participation in something like this was out of the question. She had no sense of caution, no tolerance for the desert climate, and once she'd told him about the accident and injuries she'd lived through, he felt even more protective of her. She was exactly what she said: a wimp and a wuss.

A wimp with eyes that could melt stone and a smile that could stir a monk's hormones. And damn her, what a heart. A crazy, foolhardy, impulsive heart...but bigger than the sky.

Kansas had sidled up to him, but he didn't realize it until she plucked his sleeve and motioned. "I saw the bird feeders spread across the yard, but I didn't realize they were for hummingbirds. You see those two?"

Yeah, Pax saw the hummingbird pair who had landed on the red-tagged feeder ten feet away from them—and was grateful they'd temporarily distracted Kansas from the subject of her brother. "The breed is called a frilled conquette. They got the name from the red crest on the their heads...you see how the boy is fluffing up that crest? The idea is to make him look big and ferocious—he's real hot to impress his girl."

"Well, he's doing a great job of impressing *this* girl." Kansas cupped her hand to shield her eyes from the sun. "Lord, their feathers look like diamonds in the sun. Diamonds that somehow change colors."

"If you could put one of those feathers under a microscope, you'd see it was covered with hundreds of tiny 'bubbles.' Those bubbles are of all different sizes, and that's why they seem to change color, because light bounces off them at different angles."

"Well, if that isn't a disgusting explanation. I mean—how scientific. I'd rather think it was magic." She shot him a fleeting grin, but her attention zipped back to the birds. "They're so tiny. So beautiful. So fragile."

"They're that. They're also rambunctious, mercurial and full of hell—quarrel over nothing and squabble all day."

"Those darling little birds fight?"

"They *love* fighting. They'll charge each other right in the air, wrestle and tumble for no reason at all. And nobody seems to have told them how small they are, because the damn critters have no fear. They'll attack an eagle if it goes near the nest and never think twice. They're nuts."

"Doesn't sound nuts to me. Sounds like they're protecting their young, the ones they love. That's what love and loyalty is all about, isn't it? Taking care of our own?"

"I could have guessed you'd see their side." It wasn't the first time he'd noticed the kindred spirit relationship. She was just like them. Fearless and foolhardy. Flashy and colorful, but damn fragile. And impossible to understand, because the damn woman never did one thing by the rules he understood—not the rules of safe, rational behavior. Not in life, and not with him. "There isn't a bird alive who takes more pleasure in risking its neck, and apparently for the sheer joy of doing it."

"Hmm." He didn't know why she was suddenly looking at him instead of those birds, but there was something in those soft blue eyes that made him real, real restless. And then he didn't have to worry about it, because she abruptly spun around and flew over to the table to grab her purse. "I just realized how long I've stayed—I'd better be going. I never meant to interrupt your whole work morning."

"No sweat. I was more than ready to take a break—but I *am* stuck here for a few more hours...can't leave my surgery patients. I've got an older man named Hank who helps caretake the critters whenever I'm gone, but he isn't due here until three. If you'll wait until then, I could take you over to the store where Case worked."

"That would really be helpful—if it's not inconvenient."

Convenience had nothing to do with it. He trailed her back through the house toward the front door. "Kansas." He cleared his throat. "Would you do me a favor and not check out any more psychic healers in the phone book? Or at least run an idea by me before you leap in. I haven't seen any proof yet that Case is involved in a dangerous situation, but it just makes good sense for two heads to tackle a problem. And you can't know what you could be diving into, if you go it alone."

She fished her car keys out of her purse and then looked at him. "Honestly, Pax, there's no reason to worry about me. I can handle myself. But thank you."

From nowhere, absolutely nowhere, she surged up on tiptoe and kissed him. He hadn't touched her in days. Even the most innocent and accidental physical contact in Tombstone had underlined that he needed to be careful, meticulously careful, not to stir those unpredictable hormone beasts again.

But it was as if his lips remembered hers. As if her taste and texture and unbearably soft mouth were already burned into his brain. Emotions churned awake. Not just hormones, which he could have logically understood and forgiven himself for, but the emotion of lonesomeness. Of longing and the craving to belong. And those feelings hit him as fierce and hot as a bullet.

Hummingbirds came by their name from the natural humming sound made when their feathers beat rapidly together. The way she was pressed against him, damned if he couldn't feel her heart beating just like that, so hard that his pulse was suddenly humming.

He could make love with her.

The thought shot to his brain the way ink-stained white linen—he couldn't wash it away. She would let him. She wanted him. She told him with that audaciously winsome kiss, with the shy-bold touch of her tongue, and more, with her heart beating harder than wings.

He was in control, of course. He'd never take advantage of a vulnerable woman. It was just this trick she pulled. This unreasoning, illogical magic. She could almost make him believe that he really mattered to her, that she knew him, really knew him at some damn fool soul level that no one else had ever touched. She was so sweet. So hopelessly soft. So wildly giving and open with her feelings. He'd never known a woman so crazy, so dangerous. She got him so riled up that he just didn't know *what* to do.

Kansas suddenly severed that kiss and lifted her head. Slowly she rocked back down on her heels. Her hair was on fire in the sunlight and a complete witch's tangle—had he done that? Her lips looked bruised-red and the buttons were undone at the top of her dress—dammit, had he done *that?*

His hands whipped around to rebutton her and put her back together. Or they tried to. She distracted him.

She touched his cheek and smiled, straight into his eyes. "I may just have to dare you into taking me to bed, Dr. Moore," she whispered.

Ten fingers. And every one of them abruptly turned into thumbs. If his life depended on it, he wasn't positive he could handle those buttons. "Red, are you *trying* to give me an ulcer? Or does it just come naturally?"

The comment flew right by her. She wasn't even listening. "I think it's going to happen whether I dare you or not. And I think it's going to happen soon. But not today, hmm?'' Her tone was easy, cheerful, communicating no perception whatsoever that she'd just wrung a man inside and out. ''I'll see you later.''

Pax clawed a hand through his hair as he watched her drive away, thinking that he didn't need her. He couldn't need her. She was just a stranger passing through, not of his world, as flighty as wind to his rock, as ethereal as a cloud to his unbudgable solidness. It was inconceivable that he could become attached to her in this short a time. It was unconscionable that he was even thinking about it.

That word ''need'' stuck in his mind like a sharp sliver, though, long after Kansas was out of sight. Eventually he figured out why. She needed *him.* She literally needed help finding her brother, and undoubtedly that was why chemistry bubbled up so powerfully between them. She was scared right now, and alone. Pax didn't mind being her anchor; it was a role as a man he'd always been comfortable with.

More to the point, he felt better, much better, once he'd identified who had the problem with need.

It was her. Not him.

It couldn't be him. When he cared about a woman, he'd always brought strength to the relationship—not need, not weakness. He'd sure as hell never pawn his weaknesses on someone more vulnerable than himself, and Kansas was about as vulnerable as a woman could be.

Making love with her was out of the question.

That decided, Pax released a pent-up sigh, scooped up one of the mangy cats and headed into the house.

Seven

He'd slept with her.

When Kansas first stepped into the hardware store, Pax was right behind her. She paused a second to get a feeling for the ambience of the place where her brother had worked. The store was crowded, late afternoon, and clearly one of the bright, new mode of female-friendly hardware stores where one could buy anything from nails to fancy dinnerware to African violets for the kitchen windowsill. Kansas wasn't paying much attention to the people—until the woman spotted Pax and raced over to greet him.

According to the button on her shirt, the lady was an assistant manager. Physically she was tall, willowy and buxom, with her hair done up in a classy French braid and a smile as natural as sunshine.

Kansas examined every inch of the other woman's appearance in five seconds flat. Never mind that she had no court evidence to prove Pax had had an affair with the sturdy, no-makeup and no-artifice brunette. She *knew.* The way the woman looked at Pax spoke louder than a highway billboard.

So this was the kind of woman Pax had succumbed to before, was it?

Kansas felt an instantaneous slam of both jealousy and despair. Blast and tarnation. The woman was absolutely everything that Kansas wasn't—and never would be. Worse yet, she had never been prone to envy or jealousy. That such emotions could leap so fast to her heart warned her exactly how disastrously important Pax had become in her life.

"Kansas..." When Pax realized she'd fallen a step behind him, he scooched an arm around her shoulder to bring her into the conversational fold. "This is Laney Roundtree. We've known each other for years. She didn't hire your brother, but she worked here when he did."

Laney immediately extended a hand—and another one of those disgustingly warm, genuine smiles. "Glad to meet you, Kansas. I thought a lot of your brother. We were all surprised when he suddenly stopped showing up for work—we really thought he was pretty happy here."

"I'm glad to meet you, too, and thanks." Kansas put some feminine oomph into the return handshake—and mentally kicked herself. A familiar anxiety surged through her pulse the instant Laney mentioned Case. This was just no time to be worrying about her relationship with Pax. Her brother had to be her first and only priority right now. "That's exactly why I'm here—because of my brother's disappearance. I was hoping to talk with someone he worked with, especially if there was anyone he was close to?"

"Well, you can talk to the boss—Jane Edgars runs the place, and she's the one who hired him. But you might have better luck just talking to Randy. He's one of the stock boys, used to go to lunch with Case all the time—he's in the back room right now. The sign says Employees Only, but you can just push open the door back there."

Kansas suspected that Ms. Roundtree was tickled to have a few minutes alone with Pax, but raving jealousy or no raving jealousy, she didn't mind being dismissed. Pax might not approve of her methods, but she never had a problem getting people to talk with her one-on-one. She hoped this boy might have some real answers concerning Case.

She found Randy in the back room, unloading boxes from a delivery truck, the sweat pouring from his pale face like a river. A scrawny tuft of hair stuck out of his chin. It was more than clear he wasn't going to shave that hair—it was his best manly try at a beard. He was just a boy. He had a man's shoulders, but a kid's gangling arms and legs and a face still full of pimples. He reminded her of her brother.

And he scared her half to death.

Twenty minutes later, Kansas walked blindly out of the stockroom, barely noticing where she was going until Pax abruptly clutched her shoulders. She'd nearly crashed right into him. "Hey. Are you okay?" he asked.

"Sure."

"You found the kid?"

"Yeah, and I talked to him."

His hands dropped, but he studied her face with the sharpness of a laser beam. "What happened? What'd he say?"

She didn't answer until they were out of the crowded, noisy store and back in his truck, alone. As he tooled down the highway, she pushed off her sandals and propped her bare feet on the dash, but she couldn't stop her mind from racing at a hundred miles an hour.

"All this time, I've been trying to believe that Case was involved in nothing more than tarot readings on a lazy afternoon. Something for fun, and for pete's sake, I love messing with a little mysticism and otherworld stuff myself." She sank her head against the headrest. "That Randy was just a boy. Clean-cut. Sweet. Not all that different from my brother. Only suddenly he's talking about the real existence of witches and 'dark spirits.' Purification rituals to drive out the devils and evil spirits in ourselves. How to get 'pure' and be part of nature again. And dammit, Pax, he believed what he was saying...I'm going to Nogales."

"Nogales?"

"Randy gave me a lead. A name of someone with a shop there. A guy named Miguel, supposedly a close friend of Case's. He said Nogales wasn't that far a drive, and I figured I could still head there tonight."

"You're right, it isn't a far drive. Nogales is the biggest border town from here—lots of tourists shoot down there to walk into Mexico and shop. And it's great for that, but a woman doesn't go there at night, Kansas."

She glanced at her watch, then at him. "I've taken up another one of your afternoons, haven't I? You probably have animals to take care of and a hundred things to do."

"Women don't go there alone at night," Pax repeated. "That's an automatic. It's a period. Wouldn't matter if you were a six-foot athlete with a black belt in karate. It's not safe. If you want to hit Nogales, you do it during the day."

She nodded. "Don't worry about it, Pax. I figured you got roped into plans for the evening."

"Pardon?"

"Laney. She's real pretty, seemed real nice." Kansas fixed the jangling charms on her bracelet. "I don't know how long the affair's been over, but it wasn't hard to figure out that she'd love to pick it back up again. She asked you for dinner, I'm guessing."

"Kansas..." Pax cleared his throat. "Damned if I know how this conversation moved so fast from Case and Nogales to Laney—but you're five miles off base."

"Okay."

"She's just an old friend."

"Okay."

"You didn't talk to her for five minutes. How you could come up with such wild conclusions is beyond me. She's a real nice woman and an old friend. And that's all.''

Kansas nodded soothingly. ''I guessed the affair had been over for a while. Three years?''

''Four.'' As fast as the word slipped out, Pax rolled his eyes in chagrin. ''I swear you could get blood out of a turnip. I never meant to say that.''

''Ah, well. It's just me. It's not like you're giving away crown secrets to a rival government.'' She grinned at him, then casually slipped in another question. ''So...why didn't it work?''

''Why didn't *what* work?''

''The relationship. Personally the French braid got to me. I always want to strangle women who can work all day and still not have a hair out of place. It's not normal. It's disgusting. But that was the only serious flaw I noticed.'' Kansas rearranged the charms on her bracelet. Again. ''She looked athletic and outdoorsy. I'd bet you two tuned into lots of the same channels. She seemed really grounded,, secure, comfortable with herself. It was obvious she cared about you. And you must have been attracted to that willowy look or you'd never have had the affair. So what didn't work?''

''How about if we do something really strange and heretofore never tried before—like attempt to finish one conversation at a time? The last I knew, we were talking about your *not* going to Nogales.''

''Oops. I was being nosy again, wasn't I? Prying too deep?''

''Don't waste your breath trying to sound repentant. Nothing's going to stop you from being nosy in this lifetime.''

''True,'' she admitted, ''but you certainly don't have to feel obligated to share anything with me—''

''Hell.'' Pax sighed, a loud, aggrieved, distinctly male sigh. ''I can tell we're going nowhere until you get this out of your system. *Yes*, she asked me to dinner, and *no*, I'm not going out with her. Tonight or any other night. And we ended the affair amicably. There was never any big, huge problem—she just wanted a level of closeness that I couldn't seem to give her. I tend to go off on my own, need time to myself—I told you I'm an independent type. We made good friends, but bad lovers, and that was that. Now is there anything else you want to know?''

''I'll bet *she* never poked her nose into your private business,'' Kansas murmured.

''You're right. She didn't.''

''I'll bet she never badgered you into talking about a problem, either, did she?''

"She never badgered me about anything. She was *nice*. Easy, quiet, restful to be around." He added meaningfully, "Unlike some women I know."

"Hmm. Is that what you usually go for? Willowy? Stacked? Nobody real intrusive...the kind of woman who just basically lets you alone? Nobody who's gonna stir the leaves?"

"I don't *want* the leaves stirred. I'm a peaceful man. I like a calm, quiet life. And enough is enough—you've had your twenty questions, Kansas. About your going to Nogales—"

"Well, heavens, if my going to Nogales alone bothers you that much, not to worry. I just won't go. No sweat."

There were two towns named Nogales—one on the American side of the border, the other on the Mexican side. Both towns were teaming with noises, smells and dark shadows.

Pax grabbed her arm before Kansas got mowed down by a motorcycle. They'd chosen to drive her rental car, because the Honda was small enough to squeeze into the rare parking spots near the actual border. They'd parked on the American side, but from then on, they were traveling on foot. "You hug your purse, and you stick close."

"Yes, Pax," Kansas said, and then murmured, "This is fantastic!"

Pax sighed. It was going to be a long couple of hours. She listened to his suggestions about caution about as well as she told the truth. He knew damn well she was determined to make this trip and find that cohort of her brother's. She'd have gone—and alone—if he hadn't gotten tough and insisted on coming with her.

Lights glared brightly directly at the border gates, and enough uniforms hovered around to make anyone feel secure. No American needed a passport to cross, and once through the turnstile, it was easy walking distance to the shopping district of Nogales...assuming they ever got there.

Kansas gawked with fascination at everything. The driver of a rickety truck with a precariously loaded bed full of produce screamed in Spanish about some delay. Cycles and mopeds zoomed around cars, honking and threatening all pedestrians. Peddlers hawked spicy foods from street stands, the food odors choking thick on the crowded streets.

There was nothing wrong with the place in the daytime. A lot of women called it a "shop till you drop" paradise. It was just that darkness changed the ambience. A few other things went for sale that were more conveniently hawked in shadows and dark alleys.

Once past the border itself, the real bright lights disappeared. They hadn't walked a block before Kansas started getting catcalls and invitations from passing male admirers.

"They seem to be a little short on redheads in this neck of the woods," she said dryly.

"I warned you, didn't I?" He'd suggested that she dress subdued, and in principle, she had. The navy pants and blouse were the closest to conservative he'd ever seen on Kansas, and she'd left off all jewelry, all color. But the pants snuggled to her nonexistent fanny; the blouse was open at the throat, and that carrot top of hers was always going to be a beacon.

"Are you still annoyed with me?" she asked him. "I never meant for you to feel obligated to come. I live in St. Paul, for heaven's sake. I'm no rookie about how to behave in a city."

"This isn't your average Emerald City, Toto. It's literally another country."

"If I'd thought ahead, I'd have applied a little black shoe paint to my hair," she admitted, as yet another dark-eyed Lothario whistled as she passed. "I'm beginning to feel—just an eensy bit—like a hanging rack of lamb. How far is that address to Miguel's, anyway?"

''Just a few more blocks.'' The street number for this Miguel was in the middle of the main shopping drag. The shopping district was set up like a street fair, with small booths packed together, and wares jammed and spilling into the street. The sellers stood outside, trying to entice and cajole every passerby into stopping, wildly flattering all the women who passed, promising everything they'd ever dreamed of—and a few things they hadn't.

Kansas slipped an arm around his waist, as if blithely announcing his ownership claim over this particular rack of lamb. They passed a dozen jewelry places where the shine of native silver should have given her a lust attack—God knew, she loved bangles. Other stalls displayed ceramics and leather, clothes with bright embroidery, belts, purses, rugs and wall hangings that should have aroused an orgy of spending in a bargain hunter.

She didn't even look. Her chin was cocked up and her smiles were easy, but her fingers clutched his ribs in a death grip. He knew she was anxious, even if no one else did.

As if they were old lovers, they found a gait and walking pace that adapted to their different heights. Her hip rocked against his thigh, and her scent drifted to his nostrils, warm and evocative.

He could feel the damp heat in her palm. He could feel the soft swell of her breasts rubbing his side, like a mosquito bite he couldn't itch.

The phrase "out of control" came to his mind.

Around Kansas, he thought darkly, the phrase "out of control" was becoming as familiar as his own heartbeat. She hadn't said one word about their conversation that afternoon, yet it lingered and buzzed in his head like a bee sting. His past relationships with women were an off-limits subject. Kansas had no respect for off-limits subjects. She was shamelessly nosy. She was as relentless as a hound and as stubborn as a mule. She deliberately used guilt and feminine wiles to trick a man into talking.

The entire world—every single person who knew him—picked up fast that Pax was a man who valued his privacy. Anyone with a brain, or a hair of perception, realized quickly that intrusions on his personal life were unwelcomed. Except for her.

He wasn't used to a woman who poked under his lid. And he'd known what she was getting at in that conversation about Laney. Kansas implied that he'd been picking entirely wrong women in the past, based on the criteria that they hadn't badgered him or gotten under his skin or driven him nuts. As if a man would *want* a woman who drove him nuts. As if he'd been missing something because he'd chosen to be with nice, reasonable, rational, sane women in the past.

"Pax?" Her hip stopped rocking against his. In fact, she suddenly stopped dead, right in the middle of a throng of pedestrians.

"What?"

"I'm about to get the hiccups. And I think I'm getting a blister on my right heel. And I can't seem to get my head straight about what I should say to this guy."

If there was some logic to this sequence of announcements, it eluded Pax. Either he was getting used to following her impossible conversations, or he was learning to quit listening to what she said and pay more attention to what he saw. The face tilted up to his was tense and pale. "Don't tell me you're nervous? I've seen you take on strangers right and left without a qualm."

"I'm not nervous. I'm scared to death. It's an entirely different thing. If this Miguel doesn't have answers about my brother, we're out of leads. And if he won't talk—"

"He'll talk." The traffic would just have to route around them. He bent down to kiss her. He hated to break a lifelong pattern of never indulging in an impulse, but there was no help for it.

This had nothing to do with the disturbing idea that she'd become irrationally, crazily, heartbeat important to him. This had to do with Kansas being afraid. Never mind if heat sluiced through his blood in a rush—a kiss was a sure cure for that sheet-white pallor. Color shot straight to her cheeks. So, eventually, did a smile.

"Is that your treatment for nervousness, Dr. Moore?"

"No reason for you to be nervous about this Miguel." It was too damn tempting to kiss her again. He slugged his hands into his pockets where they had no choice about behaving. "If he's living on this side of the border, I'd guess the whole conversation is likely to be in Spanish. Which means you get to sit on the sidelines. I'll handle him."

The promise was easier made than delivered, he discovered. It took a few more minutes before they located Miguel's place of business. No different than a dozen other jewelry stalls, the small space was cluttered stem to stern with racks of earrings and doodads and shiny bangles. The young man effusively greeted Kansas in Spanish, clearly anticipating a customer, but when Pax stepped in front of Kansas, Miguel turned tight-lipped.

Pax studied him carefully before even trying

to initiate some questions. The young man was around five foot five, with a scar zigzagging down the side of his chin; he looked thin and malnourished and tired. Beyond the masculine gleam in his eyes when he laid eyes on Kansas, he didn't look like trouble, more like a kid who'd seen more of the harsh side of life than he needed to.

His whole face tightened when Pax mentioned Case. He didn't know Case, he told Pax in Spanish. Never heard the name. Didn't know anything about a religious group who followed the old ways. Had never been near the Coronado area—it would have been illegal for him to cross the border—and he wasn't looking for trouble with the law.

The boy didn't lie worth beans, and Pax saw the fear and wariness spring into his eyes. Still, he'd worked with people in rescue situations dozens of times. He knew how to deal with panic. A calm, quiet response went a long way toward building reassurance and trust, but this boy wasn't budging for rock.

Kansas edged to his side, and gestured to the boy toward a trayful of earrings. There had to be a hundred pair of earrings heaped and tangled on the tray. When she had Miguel's attention, she opened the catch on her purse.

"You buy some?" Miguel asked her.

"I'll buy the whole tray...if you'll tell me about my brother." Before Pax could stop her, Kansas had lifted out her change purse and openly revealed the slip full of bills.

The boy's understanding of English was limited, but he understood money just fine. He did not immediately comprehend that she was serious about buying the entire trayful—primarily because Pax refused to translate the outlandish offer.

"Red, he's going to peg you for a sucker."

"Then he'll have me pegged right. I am a sucker." She splayed the bills in her wallet again so Miguel could clearly see them. "Just tell him it's all his, if the information he gives me about my brother is worth it."

"But that's just the point—you won't know. He could lie or make something up or tell you anything he thought you wanted to hear to get that money."

"Pax, he looks like he hasn't eaten in a week, for pete's sake. So I'm out some stupid money. So what? And it just might start him talking."

It started him talking, all right. With his eyes on those bills, the boy gushed like an open faucet for the next fifteen minutes. Once he was done—and money changed palms—he pumped Kansas's hand exuberantly and tossed one last comment to Pax. *"La mujer y las tortillas, calientes han de ser."*

"What was that last thing he said to you?" Kansas asked as they headed back down the street.

"Another one of the local proverbs. 'Women and tortillas should be hot.' If you need a further translation from that—he was remarking on my taste in women. He thought you were one irresistibly hot tamale."

"Tamale, huh?" She chuckled. "I thought you looked a little ticked off."

Ticked off didn't quite measure Pax's mood. As they ambled back toward the border, Kansas was a hundred pair of earrings—and a tray—richer. And Pax had a fresh bucketful of information about the place known as *Valle de Oro* where this group regularly camped in the Coronado—but no possible way of knowing how much of Miguel's story was true.

"Just so we get this straight for now and for all times—I'm never taking you to Vegas," he told her.

"Now, Pax. There's a time and a place to bluff, but I didn't think this was it. We were getting nowhere. I could see he didn't want to talk. Even if he embellished or exaggerated anything he said—even if he invented stuff—at least it gave us something to work with. He knew Case. I could see it in his face the instant you mentioned my brother's name.''

''I agree about that. He knew your brother.''

''So what did he say? Are you going to keep me in suspense? I picked up some words—like Coronado and Sierra Vista and *Valle de Oro*—but that's about all I could understand.'' When Pax didn't immediately answer, Kansas pounced again. ''Tell me! Everything! He was talking to beat the band for all that time—''

''Yeah, I know. And I'll tell you what he said word for word,'' Pax said slowly, ''if you promise to take it with a long, slow grain of salt. No making decisions. No rushing into action. No doing anything half-cocked based on what a half-grown boy probably made up, just to get your money.''

''Pax, Pax, Pax.'' Kansas sprang up on tiptoe and smacked him, right on the lips. The devil of a kiss was a total contradiction to the sincerity in her eyes. ''As if I were the type to do anything impulsive. Trust me. All I'm going to do is listen.''

Eight

They were home from Nogales—Pax had just driven off and Kansas had just tossed her purse on the counter—when the telephone rang.

She grabbed the portable phone from the kitchen, and crooked the receiver between her ear and shoulder. She should have expected the call from her mom. They hadn't talked since the day before yesterday.

"No, no, I was just out for a couple of hours, Mom. With Dr. Moore. I told you about him. No, sweetie, you know I'd have called if I had any real news. And you promised to let me do the worrying, remember? That's why I'm here..."

Her voice was deliberately calm and soothing, but her hands were working faster than a card shark, yanking open drawers all through the kitchen. She wanted maps. Not *regular* maps—she already had dozens of those. But when Pax talked to Miguel, she'd heard the name *'Valle de Oro'* crop up yet again. If her brother was anywhere, it was with those kids. And if Case had found his way to that place in the Coronado, surely he had maps or directions or some kind of information lying around somewhere.

"No, Mom, I haven't laid eyes on him yet, but I believe I know where he is now..." Leaving the drawers gaping open, she jogged in the living room and started pilfering through the desk and bookshelves.

"Now, sweetie, I know you're upset and concerned. So am I. And I'm not going to lie and tell you everything's hunky dory. But when I first got here, I was really scared that he'd disappeared because he was lying in a ditch somewhere. It's not like that. I think he's fine. I have no reason to believe he's physically injured, nothing like that...I bought you some earrings tonight, in fact—now would I be goofing off shopping if I thought something bad had happened to Case?"

In a crisis, her mom could handle anything and

probably reorganize a government or two in her spare time. But she was a hand-wringing worrier, Kansas knew. If and when Case needed the family's help, she'd tell the truth straight and knew her mom would come through like a trooper. Until then, she figured it was a daughter's job to reassure rather than scare. Protecting her mom was such a familiar habit that it required no concentration—a good thing, because her mind was spinning in a thousand other directions right now.

"Mom, I don't *know.* I believe he's gotten involved with a group of kids. Other young people his age. And I'm almost positive that's where he is—camping out with this group—but I'll be able to tell you for sure in a couple of days..."

Deserting the mess in the living room, she sprinted down the hall. What the Sam Hill did she need for a hike in the mountains, anyway? In Case's bedroom, she opened and slammed drawers, tossing T-shirts and shorts onto the bed, then flew to the closet. On the floor in the back, she found a terrific pair of hiking boots. Serious, practical hiking boots—but size twelve. About as helpful as a mink coat in the desert.

The doorbell rang just as she was scooching back out of the closet. She glanced at the bedside clock—11:00 p.m.? Pax had only left a few minutes before, and no one in town knew her well enough to call, not this late. Unless—she lurched quickly to her feet and hustled toward the front door—it was someone or something about her brother.

"Mom, I have to go. Someone's here. I don't know who it is—I just heard the doorbell...let me call you back tomorrow, okay? Now, Mom, you've got to stop this...you're going to worry yourself sick, imagining all these dire things—*real* people don't have amnesia, come on now...I promise, the instant I know anything for sure about Case, I'll call—"

Still holding tight to the phone, she squinted through the peephole in the front door, and raised her eyebrows when she identified Pax. Her pulse instantly zoomed to a polka. Heaven knew why he'd come back, but she quickly yanked open the door.

When he stepped in, she motioned to the phone. He nodded in understanding. "Mom, I'll call you tomorrow, I promise, cross my heart and hope to die, but I really have to go now. I love you, too. And give Mike a big kiss. Yeah, I'm taking care of myself. Yeah, I'm eating—*Mom!* Good night!"

With a phew of a sigh, she punched the Off

button and pivoted around—but Pax was no longer in sight.

She was vaguely aware that she'd torn through the house so fast in the last few minutes that the place must look like a disaster area. Apparently Pax noticed, because he was standing in the living room with his palms jammed into his back pockets, perusing the upended desk drawers and debris with a scowl.

"What happened? Did you forget something?"

"Yeah." He turned around and aimed that scowl at her. "I almost forgot that I couldn't trust you."

She arched a brow. "I've got news for you, buster. You can trust me with your life."

Pax rolled his eyes. "That's not the kind of trust that was in question, Red. I didn't get five miles down the road before I realized you were just too calm and reasonable after that confrontation with Miguel. I had a feeling you were selling me a wooden nickle—and a real fear you'd do something fast and impulsive." He motioned to the clutter scattered all over the room.

"If you're implying I'm freaked out...you're damn right I am."

"So how come you weren't honest with me?"

"Because I didn't figure you'd agree. Or that

you'd like what I was going to do. I don't need to talk to any more people, Pax. I've heard more than enough to be scared witless about my brother. I think there's a time to be rational, and a time when getting hysterical is perfectly appropriate. I'm going up in those mountains to find him. Don't waste your breath arguing with me."

He didn't waste his breath arguing. He disappeared on her, and showed up a few moments later with a jelly glass splashing full of whiskey. "Your brother," he said, "didn't put a lot of money into the brand. It'll probably give you a headache after two sips. Drink it anyway, Red. *De decir y hacer hay mucho que ver.*"

"What's that mean?"

"It means that unfortunately, there's much to do between saying and doing. No matter what harebrained thing you plan to do, it's still going to take some time and effort to put together. You can be as hysterical as you want, shorty—but you might as well sip that whiskey while you're talking it out."

Possibly Pax had noticed that she had slightly exaggerated her state of mind. She wasn't the least bit hysterical. She wished she were, though. She wished she were in a mood to vent a full-fledged, loud, unreasonable, and immature tantrum.

Instead she sank onto the couch and took a throat-tearing sip of the acrid whiskey. It helped. She couldn't remember being this scared. Pax had been wonderful with Miguel; she doubted the boy even realized he was being grilled, and once the subject veered toward religion, the young man had seemed to need to express his feelings and beliefs.

By the time Pax translated the conversation on the drive home, Kansas knew he'd colored it—the same way she colored the truth for her mother to protect her. But she'd spent hours with Case's books and papers over the past week. Clues clicked in place, and connected with things she already knew.

Religion wasn't the problem. Drugs combined with religion was the problem. The Aztecs had a word for *datura—ololiuhqui.* The Spanish used their own word for the plant—*toloache.* The Zunis, Pueblo, and Navajo people had a history of using the plant in long ago eras. Not now. Now anyone with a brain realized that it was a dangerous hallucinogen with narcotic properties.

"Now, don't go quiet on me," Pax said gently. "Talk. Spill out what's on your mind."

She looked at him, but she simply couldn't talk. The lump in her throat was as thick as a wall. The things he'd relayed from Miguel kept springing into her mind. In the old days, a bit of the narcotic was placed in a person's food or water to induce visions. The purpose wasn't getting high. It was getting pure. If the person saw devils, it was because he needed to get rid of the bad spirits inside him. Datura was supposed to cleanse and purify the soul.

Miguel had said that initiates were given the drug as a "rite of passage." It was a test, to see how they coped. Outsiders didn't understand. It wasn't about doing something illegal or playing with party drugs. It wasn't about rebellion. It was about wanting and needing to dig deep inside yourself for the "real truth."

The real truth? Oh, God. When Kansas had found a medical text and looked up jimsonweed, the more common name for datura, it was listed as poisonous. It had some potent alkaloid called atropine. A misdose could be fatal. The hallucinogenic and narcotic properties of the damn thing were just as terrifying.

And the thought that her brother could be involved in something like that was enough to make Kansas violently ill. Case too easily trusted, she knew well. No different than Miguel, he could actually believe he was taking some harmless "natural herb" if that's what his friends told him.

"Talk about a way to scare a man," Pax murmured. "When you get quiet, Red, I know we're in big trouble."

"I just...I just can't wait, Pax. Not another day. Not another minute. Both that psychic and Miguel mentioned this same *'Valle de Oro.'* I'm not denying what you said—trying to explore the whole Coronado just to find this sacred place would be crazy. But I don't care. It's not only the best lead we have, but it also adds up with everything else. There *has* to be a way to find the place. I'm going after my brother."

"Nope, you're not."

"This isn't up to you, love." She didn't mean the endearment to slip out. She guessed that Pax didn't want to hear it, and this was just no time to deal with either the complications—or the wonder—of falling in love with him. "This isn't up to you," she repeated quietly. "It's up to me. He's my brother."

"I understand that. But before doing anything, I think you should talk to the sheriff again." He raised a hand when she started to object. "Just hear me out. We can be sitting on the sheriff's doorstep first thing in the morning, Kansas. Before dawn, if you want. You sure as hell couldn't do anything before then anyway, now could you?"

"No." Although she hated admitting it.

"I'm just suggesting that we lay out everything we've learned in front of the sheriff. I know you were frustrated when you talked to him before—and maybe Simons still can't do anything. Your brother isn't breaking any laws by camping with a bunch of kids, and we don't have a lick of proof that he's in any danger. But I know Simons. He'll at least listen, and if nothing else, he may have heard some more things about this group than he could tell us. You want to risk that not happening?"

"No."

The starch seeped out of Pax's shoulders when he realized she was agreeing with him. Still, his eyes studied hers sharply. "So we'll talk to the sheriff...but no matter what he says, you can relax, Red, because I'll go. It's been a while since I hiked that whole area, but I know those mountains. It'll take me some time to clear my decks, get some gear together, and make arrangements with Hank to take care of the place. But whether I agree with you or not—whether I think this is a damn fool idea or not—I'll go. I'll find this *Valle de Oro,* and if your brother is anywhere around there, I'll find him. That's a promise. You hear me?"

"Yes," she murmured, feeling overwhelmed,

as if something inside was taking fragile, soaring wing. Pax was taking her side, even when he obviously disagreed with her. He couldn't know what a gift that was. All her adult life, she'd never found a man who took her seriously. It was too easy to ignore the opinion of a pint-size female. Pax respected her point of view even if it wasn't his own.

"So..." Pax was still studying her warily. "We're agreed on a plan? We'll see the sheriff in the morning—and you won't try to do anything tonight."

"I promise not to do anything tonight," Kansas said sincerely. She had no problem agreeing to that part of his plan. There was only one small detail that she disagreed with, but that would wait until later. Right now, they might as well both get a good night's sleep. There was no purpose in upsetting Pax until she had to.

He hated getting upset, she knew. He wasn't the tantrum type. He was the never-get-roiled-up-and-blow-your-cool type. She suspected that he expressed anger by going cold, instead of hot. And he'd probably get ultraquiet instead of loud.

Well, she'd find out tomorrow.

"Dammit!" The morning was serenely quiet and peaceful—until Pax slammed the Explorer's

door loud enough to make the truck shake. "You're not going, Kansas!"

"Now, no reason to get your liver in an uproar. You don't have to take me with you. I can either follow you or just do the trip on my own. Do you want a doughnut? I have some fresh glazed ones in the kitchen—"

"*No,* I don't want any damn doughnut!"

"Well, come on inside, anyway. A nice, tall glass of ice tea will calm you down."

"I *am* calm!" Pax had never lost his temper with a woman. Even if a woman was driving him to drink, losing his temper would have been unconscionable. Inconceivable. Nothing he would ever let happen. "I am completely calm," he repeated. "You're the one who isn't thinking calmly and clearly."

"Actually I'm thinking quite clearly," she said amiably, and darted ahead of him toward the kitchen. By the time he'd followed, she'd taken a chunk out of a glazed doughnut and was plopping ice cubes into two glasses. She retrieved a pitcher of golden tea from the fridge and *thunked* the door closed with her hip. "We both guessed how the visit with the sheriff was going to go, didn't we? Not that he wasn't real patient and sweet. Speaking of which—do you want sugar in your tea?"

"No."

"Why did I bother asking," she murmured, "I should have known you wouldn't go in for an indulgence like sugar…but back to Simons—I honestly understand why he's unwilling to do anything. He just doesn't see why I'm worried. My brother is of age, living independently and Case had no obligation to check in with family before taking off for a while. He'd done it before. Simons was more than willing to run his name through the system, check the hospitals and all that, but he just doesn't have the resources or manpower to search the mountains without some reason to believe Case is in danger. The sheriff is just dead positive I'm being an overprotective sister. But even so…"

Her voice faded when she disappeared around the corner, apparently expecting Pax to follow her into the living room. He stomped after her. She set the glasses down, flopped on the couch and fluffed the pillow with a gesture for him to sit next to her. Pax didn't want to sit. He wanted to throttle her. In between bites of the glazed doughnut, she was still chattering on like a cheerful magpie.

"Even so, at least he listened about the datura. He'd heard about the kids camping out and the religion thing before, Pax. You could see it in his face. But he hadn't heard about any drugs being involved. I think he'd take action quickly if we came across real evidence that those kids were messing with hallucinogens. Of course, that's of no immediate help to my brother—"

"Kansas, there's no reason for you to rehash the whole visit. I heard everything he said. I was right there. And I told you I'd go into the mountains and find your brother. *Alone.* We agreed—"

"I never agreed that I wasn't going with you," she said gently.

"Don't give me that bullcracky. It was *understood* that I would go alone."

"You may have understood that, love. But I'm just not the type to sit home and knit socks while my guy goes off to war. This isn't even your war. It's my brother's and my problem."

Pax sucked in a lungful of patience and tried again. "The blood relationship has nothing to do with it. Kansas—listen to me. I know the general country we're talking about. Nothing is easy. Even my Jeep will only get us so far, and there are places too steep for horses—so we're talking about hiking. We're talking about walking over hilly, rugged terrain for hours in the hot sun. We're talking about camping overnight in the rough. We're talking your worst nightmare, Red."

"It sure sounds like it," she agreed. "Honestly, though, you don't have to yell. I can hear you just fine."

He was not yelling. If his voice was projecting at the volume of a thundering boom, it was because nothing less seemed to penetrate his redhead's bullheaded skull. "You're not listening to me."

"Actually I am."

"I've done this kind of thing a hundred times alone. There's just no reason for you to be involved—"

"There could be. If we find this group—and my brother—he might not want to leave." If Kansas hadn't voiced the fear before, the haunted look in her eyes illustrated how deeply the problem had weighed on her mind. "I don't know how much influence this group has had on him, or if drug use could have affected his personality. But you'd be going into the situation cold, Pax, a total stranger to him. I know Case. If he'll listen to anyone, he'll listen to me."

Pax paced the length of the room—for the third time. A fleeting, disturbing image flashed through his mind of what being married to her would be like—and her using that blue velvet voice every time she wanted to win an argument. It was an unreasonable female tactic. And utterly distracting. "I recognize that's a potential problem, but I'll find a way to handle your brother. That's not the issue. The issue is that you don't have the stamina to handle a trip in the desert. And I'm not about to take you into a situation where you could be hurt."

"You think I'll hold you back and slow you down," she announced. "Well, that's certainly true. I understand that I'd be a royal pain in the fanny to take along—and it's okay. We don't have to pair up even-steven. I'll just follow behind you."

Hell, the thought of her wandering around the mountains alone almost blew the volcano top off his blood pressure. "No. I'm through arguing. You're not going. Period."

"Yeah," she said gently, "I am."

She'd just taken a quick sip of that iced tea when she deliberately put it down again. He was standing by the sliding doors when she uncoiled from the couch and lurched to her feet. Barefoot, she ambled toward him with a slow, easy gait as if she were strolling in a park. She wasn't smiling, but the look in her eyes was confoundingly...warm. "You know what?"

"What?"

"This is the first time you've been mad at me. I mean, *really* mad. It's okay, did you notice? I was beginning to wonder if you'd ever trust me enough to take off your manners and express something you were really feeling. You don't have to be in control every second. Not with me."

"Kansas, I have a real low tolerance for psycho-babble and I don't have a clue what you're talking about, so if you're trying to distract me—"

"I am. I definitely am. But I'm also trying to tell you that I'm proud of you."

Proud of him for losing his temper and bellowing at the top of his lungs at her? Pax thought understanding Kansas was like trying to understand a powder puff.

And then the powder puff lifted her arms, reached up behind his head and—totally bewildering him—undid the leather thong that held back his hair. "What are you *doing?*"

"Expressing what I feel. For you." She tossed the leather string behind her. Then lifted on tiptoe, and burrowed her slim white fingers into his hair. "It would just get in your way if it wasn't pulled back, wouldn't it? But I wondered what it would feel like loose. It's so thick. Like ink against my skin. Coarse, not soft—"

"I know what you're doing—you're trying to drive me crazy. You think if you start talking like this, I'll completely forget about your brother—"

"The issue about my brother was settled five minutes ago, Pax. The feelings between us haven't been settled at all, and I'm afraid this just won't wait any longer." She immediately tempered that warning. "Of course, you can always stop me."

She tugged his head down to kiss him. She tasted like sweet, sugary doughnut crumbs. She tasted like every woman he'd ever wanted, every fantasy lover he'd ever dreamed of. Her tongue was soft and wet and wanton, and suddenly he couldn't catch his breath.

It was so like his hummingbird to do nothing by the rule book. She knew he was furious with her. And it was midmorning. And they were in the middle of her brother's living room, with sun beaming through the glass doors. The place and time were so contrary to any ambience of desire that naturally he was thrown off balance. He couldn't possibly have anticipated that Kansas was going to choose this instant to cause him trouble.

That didn't quite explain, though, how the scent of her went straight to his head. It didn't explain the sudden drumming in his ears, as if he'd just taken a dive under dark, dark waters. It didn't explain why his mouth latched onto hers, finding her tongue, meeting it, taking it, as if kissing her back made more sense than anything he'd ever done.

Her fingers pulled at his T-shirt, yanking it free from his jeans. Soft, pampered palms stole over his bare skin, skimming over ribs and sides and winding around his back. Her hands were hot and damp from nerves. She was badly nervous, as nervous as he'd ever seen her, but that didn't inhibit her from taking him apart at the seams, one inch of skin at a time, strewing a path of firelit hormones in her wake.

Eventually she eased free from that kiss, but she stayed close, so close that her sough of a sigh whispered right next to his mouth. "I'm awfully tired of trying to kiss you standing up, big guy. You're really annoyingly tall," she murmured.

He knew what she was suggesting. He said, "No."

"If you're worried about protection, I bought some. Days ago. Right after we got wrapped up in a clinch the last time. Right when I realized I was way, way over my head. But I'm afraid the package is all the way in the bedroom—"

He repeated, "No."

She echoed her earlier offer. "You can, of course, stop me. I've never seduced anyone before, never even wanted to. I'll probably do it wrong. You already know I'm a wimp and a wuss, and I'm scared of just about everything—especially of taking big, terrifying risks like this one. So if you want me to behave myself, you can call this off real easily. Just say you don't want me."

Maybe if the blood hadn't been slamming so hard in his veins, he could have pulled off that lie. Maybe lying would have been the best thing, for her, for him. But he couldn't look in those vulnerable blue eyes and deny what he felt for her.

He took her mouth, aching hard and completely, because he couldn't believe the bewildering woman could conceivably feel insecure about how much he wanted her. She seemed to catch that message just fine, because she responded like smoke for his personal fire. Her arms wound around his neck and he felt himself lifting her. Her legs wrapped around his waist and she closed her eyes.

The bedroom was at the end of the far hall. He was lucky to get her there without injuring them both. Her hands framed his scalp and her lips clung to his with abandon, with trust he'd never earned, with more emotion pouring from her than he could believe was meant for him. His hip crashed against a wall. He pushed off one leather sandal in the hall, jettisoned the other in the bedroom doorway, grazed a shoulder against the doorjamb. Still, he kissed her. Not one, but a frenzy of kisses so deep, so rich, that they should have appeased even a starving man's hunger. Instead they aroused a blaze of hunger and a thirst for her that no mere kisses could begin to quench.

Sunlight streamed on an unmade double bed with chocolate brown sheets. They smelled like her perfume. He caught a fleeting glimpse of a bare, bald bedroom with sparse furnishings and a rented room's coldness. She'd still made it hers. There were wisps of lace and color on the straight chair. Bangles and baubles cluttering the dresser top. Blankets tangled and dragging the floor—no way Kansas would sleep neat and tame, not when nothing else was tame about her.

Her eyes never opened when he dropped her onto the bed, but her fingers wrestled with his belt buckle when he followed her down. Her green T-shirt peeled off easier than the skin on a peach. The white shorts and slinky panties stripped off just as fast. It took thirty seconds—an eternity—for him to shed his own clothes, and another eternity to get a coherent word from her about the location of the protection. Once he took care of that, he applied every ounce of concentration he could beg, muster or steal, on taking care of her.

Her eyes were blurry and dazed, her lips softer than silk. He'd known from the moment he met her that she was precious. More fragile than sunlight, more crushable and hurtable than anyone he knew. He found skin more translucent than ivory. He found freckles. He found jagged webs of pale scars from the accident she'd been through, badges of pain she'd endured, reminders of how physically frail she could be. He found small, exquisitely sensitive breasts with dark rose tips that tightened and shone under the wash of his tongue.

He meant to show her how beautiful he saw her. He meant to treat her with infinite patience and care. Control had always come so easily to him, and he had every intention of putting his own needs at bay, but Kansas...

Her fingers sieved in his hair, and between kisses, between slippery, wild caresses, she whispered to him. Her voice was husky and low, a siren calling her mate, a woman on fire cajoling for more fuel, a lady complaining about frustration that she was most unreasonably blaming him for. She wanted speed. She wanted the rush of a luge. She touched him with need, as if he were the only man in the entire universe, and he couldn't catch a breath, couldn't catch a grip, couldn't remember a moment in his life when she hadn't meant everything to him.

It was insanity. He recognized that, but only vaguely, on some distant intellectual plane that had nothing to do with that sun-dusted bed and her slim white body beneath him. Emotions engulfed him, nameless, unrecognized, no feelings he'd met up with before. They had her name on them. That was all he knew.

Her body was slick and damp when he took her, those slim legs noosed around his waist, his manhood sheathed so deeply inside her that there was no difference between her body and his. He was no stranger to intimacy, no stranger to the response of a woman's body or anything about natural, physical sexual feelings. But nothing was the same with her. Nothing was what he'd known.

She was so free, in a way he'd never understood or felt freedom, her heart naked in her eyes and both desire and need given to him like open, vulnerable gifts. Her fierce responsiveness spurred his own, spurred speed and a blinding burst of urgency. Some crazy instinct surged from nowhere, a fleeting fear that she could disappear if he wasn't careful, that he'd lose something unbearable if he lost her. His heartbeat was suddenly hammering, hammering...but then the foolish, fleeting thought was gone.

She called his name again, and he came to her. His redhead wasn't about to disappear on him. She was right there, greedy and wild and making no secret of what she wanted. They rode the fire, teasing the flames to rise and engulf them both. He lost his head. He lost his heart. And then the lap of flame and desire spun them both into oblivion.

Nine

Kansas's eyes fluttered open. Spanking bright sunlight poured through the window, revealing a scene of appalling decadence. Clothes were strewn all over the place. Sheets and pillows lay heaped and abandoned on the floor. And her bare naked body—in the middle of the day!—was intimately, brazenly tangled with Pax's bare naked body.

Drowsily she tested her conscience for guilt or shame, and found none. Not even a shred.

When she turned her head and looked at Pax, a velvet glove squeezed around her heart. He was napping. Short, thick eyelashes shadowed his cheeks, and his dark hair was hopelessly disheveled. He looked like a man recovering from a train wreck, and Kansas knew intimately well why he needed rest.

They hadn't had sex. They'd made love. And though she'd realized she was in love with him long before this, finding the wonder and richness of a man who truly touched her soul was brand-new. And her brave, strong man who never lost control had been like a stallion freed from a captive stall, wild, vulnerable, emotion exploding from him as if he'd never discovered freedom before. He'd bared his need—for her, with her. And he'd been as helpless as she.

Kansas knew how unalike they were. She knew, as soon as they found her brother, that she would lose any excuse to stay in Arizona. She knew all the reasons why making love with him should have been a mistake, yet there were no regrets in her heart or her head. Pax had been as lonely and closed up as a tomb when she met him. If he never loved her—if he never felt an ounce of the heart-soft painfully vulnerable feelings she had for him—she could never have walked away. Not without giving a gift that was within her to give. Not without touching a man who so fiercely, badly needed touching.

His short, stubby lashes swept up. In those few seconds when he seemed disoriented and still drugged-sleepy, she took advantage. She climbed on top of his chest and pinned him with a sun-warmed, whisper-soft kiss. So easily, so naturally, his mouth yielded under hers that she was tempted to spoil him with a dozen more.

But she could feel his muscles suddenly tighten with tension. And her lover might happen to arouse faster than a firecracker, but Pax came awake and aware of reality all too quickly. Intense, grave lines showed up on his forehead. Guilt darkened his eyes, eyes that searched her face as if he half believed she were a fantasy and their making love was the shock of a dream.

She told herself that was precisely the reaction she expected from him. One act of making love was hardly going to change a man who'd spent a lifetime shuttering away his emotions. Pax was never going to forgive himself easily for doing anything so disgustingly human as needing someone else. And if loving him meant anything, it meant freeing him from any association of guilt—at least with her.

"So," she murmured, "how was your day?"

He looked startled, but then he chuckled. His big callused hand swept slowly down her back in a languid, tender caress, but she wasn't fooled that he was really relaxed. ‘‘I don’t know. Did we just get hit with an earthquake?’’

‘‘I certainly did. And you’re certainly looking destroyed. There seems evidence all over the place that something powerful happened around here.’’ She propped an elbow by his shoulder. ‘‘I meant to ask you ahead of time how you felt about skinny.’’

‘‘Personally, I don’t think there’s anything more sexually exciting than skinny.’’

‘‘Good answer, big guy.’’ She pushed a thick lock of hair off his brow. ‘‘I also meant to ask you ahead of time how you felt about scars. Afraid I have some doozies left over from that accident.’’

‘‘I am extremely fond of doozy-type scars.’’

‘‘Another good answer.’’ She beamed approval for his tact—but she wasn’t through with him yet. ‘‘I also meant to ask you ahead of time if you were a breast man. I’m no Mae West. Which I realize you already knew. But geezle beezle, we definitely hadn’t been this close before, and you were doomed to a major disappointment if you had any illusions about—’’

‘‘Red?’’

‘‘Hmm?’’

He kissed her eyelids, then the tip of her nose. ‘‘There is nothing about you that could disappoint me in a month of Sundays. And I'm not sure, but I think that horse is already out of the barn. If you look down, I believe you'll discover that it's a little late to get nervous about being naked together.''

''I already looked down. And I'm not the least nervous about *you* being naked. I am insanely crazy about your body. It is a gorgeous male body. Prizewinning hunk material.''

''No one,'' Pax said wryly, ''has ever called me a hunk.''

''Well, it's about time then. And you should have had more brains than to date women who didn't appreciate you. You're irresistible. Trust me on this.''

''Could we divert this conversation to something a little more serious?''

''More serious than how gorgeous your body is?''

''Kansas.'' He touched the beating pulse in the hollow of her throat. From the look in his eyes, he hadn't been fooled by her teasing—or by her. ''I never meant to be rough,'' he said gruffly.

''You weren't. You were wonderful.''

''I was damn fast, and I'm a hundred pounds bigger than you are, and I showed all the finesse of a bull.''

She raised her eyebrows. ''Well, you're entitled to your opinion. But I was there. Participating actively, as I recall. I don't believe either one of us were really in the mood for finesse."

For an instant humor sparkled in his eyes. "May you never learn finesse, Red. And I sure as hell hope you always feel free to do anything you want around me." The humor died, replaced by something softer, quieter, darker in his eyes. "But I shouldn't have lost control."

"You're so right. How dare you be human, Doc? How dare you have needs just like anybody else? Personally I think we should skip the trial and hang you on the spot." She wooed another smile from him—but it didn't last long.

"I think you've got a few reasons to hang me," he said. "This shouldn't have happened. You've been running on anxiety and stress because of your brother. So maybe you needed someone, and maybe I was here. But you're going home in a hell of a short time—which I knew. Somehow I don't think you go to bed with anyone lightly, and to add an emotional complication to your plate—it wasn't right."

The sudden lump in her throat felt thicker than glue. "I've never gone to bed with anyone lightly," she agreed. "As beautiful as this skinny, scarred body is, it seems to take a mountain for me to trust a man with it. Truth is, the only time I ever went near a man's bed was if I were messily, stickily in love. That would sure be a nightmare, though, wouldn't it, Doc? If I fell in love with you?''

She saw the sudden stillness in his expression, and swallowed hard. No, he didn't want to hear that she'd fallen in love with him. And she could have sworn she had no illusions about their future together. She could have sworn that she had knowingly chosen the risk and joy of loving him, no matter what his feelings were for her. But damnation, the sword-sharp ache in her heart ripped at all those lies she'd been telling herself.

''Well, you don't have to worry.'' She smiled brightly. ''I'm not about to cause you any messy complications, Pax, but I want you to know—making love was no impulse and no mistake. Not for me. And there are reasons why I thought this was right...reasons that stem back to when you told me about your father.''

''My father? What on earth does he have to do with this?''

''Well, nothing. Directly. But when you told me about your dad, that was the first time I'd ever felt that someone else on this planet understood what I'd been through. When your father deserted ship, didn't you feel overwhelmed by feelings of anger and hurt?''

He went real still. ''I don't understand what you're getting at.''

''I've been down that exact same road,'' she said softly. ''After the accident, I felt so overwhelmed by feelings of anger that it scared me. I hated being helpless. I was in a rage this had happened to me, when I hadn't done one thing to deserve it. I was angry that something could tear up my life that I had absolutely no control over. You know exactly what those emotions feel like, don't you?''

''Kansas—''

She laid a fingertip on his lips, unwilling to let him interrupt. Not yet. ''After that, I decided I wanted to be an island. I wanted to be strong and invulnerable. If I couldn't control fate, I could sure as hell control *me.* So I bottled up all my feelings and tried to shut down my heart. I came up with the darnedest problem, though, Doc. I discovered that when you shut down like that—if you never take a risk and trust someone—you never give them a chance to be there for you.''

Pax cleared his throat. ''Are you...um...subtly trying to give me a lecture, Red?''

She lifted her brows. ''Heavens, no. I wasn't talking about you, big guy, I was talking about me. I was trying to explain why I made love with you—it's that rare that I find someone I can trust, really trust and feel safe with. But that trust doesn't come with strings, it just comes with understanding. You never had to worry about messy complications with me, Pax. I learned the same life lesson you did. No one can love you. Unless you open the door and let them."

She watched him absorb that idea for a moment—his eyes studied hers, his forehead etched with a frown of concentration. But when he started to respond, she swiftly bounced off his chest and climbed out of bed. "Kansas...hey, where you going?"

"We can't talk about love all day, Doc." Her voice was light, but her heart felt thick and heavy. She had told him no lies. Pax was free, and she wanted him to believe he had no obligation or responsibility because of making love with her. Caging a man was no way to love him.

He'd battened down the emotional hatches every time she'd come close before. Pax was as wary as a porcupine about anyone who came close, and Kansas understood perfectly well why she was probably the worst risk on earth for him. Still, those beautiful, fathomless dark eyes saw too much—and not enough. Allowing him to see how deeply she cared could only make him feel protective and responsible and obligated—not what she wanted from him at all.

"I don't know why you're flying around the room at the speed of sound, Red, but we're not done with this conversation."

She paused in the doorway, but only long enough to flash him a brilliant smile. "Sure we are. As exquisitely and unforgettably wonderfully as you took me out this morning, Dr. Moore…time's awasting. I'm going to hit the shower, throw together some lunch and then pack."

"Pack?"

"You didn't forget, did you? I'm going with you after Case." The urgency and need to find her brother had never been far from her mind. Now, though, she felt an urgency for herself as well. Most of her life, she'd had to be so emotionally strong that she never doubted her ability to handle trial or trouble. With Pax, she seemed to be shooting straight for heartbreak. If there was no controlling her feelings for him, it was best she get away from him, fast and soon. "If you're worried about my holding you back, Pax—don't. Trust me, I'll keep up with any pace you set. I won't cause you any problems in any way."

* * *

She couldn't keep up if her life depended on it. When Pax realized she'd fallen behind again, he stopped, dropped his backpack to the ground and waited.

Although Kansas had been gung ho hot to take off on this venture into the Coronado, in reality he'd had two days to talk her out of it. Rearranging his work schedule and planning supplies took time—just not enough time. A century of solid arguing couldn't dent that redhead's determination when she had her mind set. He gave her credit. She didn't nag. She just cajoled and bribed and teased until a man gave in from sheer exhaustion.

Pax rolled his shoulders, his eyes peeled on the twisting, steep path below. If she didn't show in another minute, he'd backtrack to find her.

A red-tailed hawk soared overhead, backdropped by a hot white-blue sky. The terrain was rough, with sharp hills and canyon-squeezed paths and unpredictable footing around every corner. Scrub trees and brush grew as impenetrably as a thicket in places, yet there was little growth tall enough to provide shade from the baking sun. Still, this was cupcake-easy country compared to many areas of the desert he'd explored. Any risk of danger could be reduced with some basic common sense and caution. He would never have taken Kansas otherwise—no matter how lethally she'd poured on the feminine wiles.

He frowned when she still failed to show. He'd only left her alone once, parking her in a shady overhang to rest while he'd gone ahead to scout the area around *Valle de Oro.* He came within a mile of where he suspected the kids might be camped and determined exactly where they were going to spend the night. Leaving her alone, though, had been a mistake. He'd found her with a full-blown case of the heebie jeebies over a seven-foot-long grayish-blueish snake she'd claimed to see.

Pax knew of no "grayish-blueish" snake species in this neck of the woods—much less any that grew to such epic lengths. Didn't matter. He wasn't leaving her alone again. As he knew too well, the lady had the potential to both find and create trouble faster than the flip of a dime.

He was braced to take off after her when, finally, a bouncing red mop showed over the rise. A sweat-damp face with a shiny nose appeared, followed by a droopy T-shirt hanging as limp as a dishrag over rag-tail cutoff shorts. His shrimp was huffing and puffing harder than the big bad wolf. "I'm coming. I'm coming. People do this for sport, huh? They actually hike this kind of country for *fun?*''

''Now just take your pack off and sit down a minute, Red.''

''The last time I sat down, a tarantula crawled out from under a rock. No, thank you. I'm not sitting down again until we get back home.''

''Just one more hour until we get to the place where we're going to stop for the night.'' He dug a tube of zinc cream from his pocket—which she saw.

''I've already got five pounds of that on my face,'' she objected.

''Yeah, well you rubbed all five pounds off. Again. Stand still.'' She lifted her face for him. Even this late in the afternoon, her ivory skin couldn't survive the sun. Kansas had bought some pansy sunscreen that wouldn't protect her worth squat. Still, he only dabbed a streak of the white cream over her nose and cheeks. The physical contact was minimal, yet his pulse suddenly bucked harder than a frisky colt.

''I think you *like* making me look like a ghoul.'' She camped a witch-face to make him chuckle. ''Pretty scary, huh?''

She scared him, all right, but it had nothing to do with the white zinc paint on her cheeks. Standing this close, it was her eyes he noticed.

Those soft, endless blue eyes and the way she looked at him—with desire, with a woman's sensual awareness, and dammit. With love.

As sure as his heartbeat, Kansas had lied to him. She'd laughed at the whole idea of being messily, stickily in love, but Pax would have to be blind and drugged to miss all the signals. The emotion was naked on her face. So was her vulnerability. And a woman didn't make love the way she had, not based on chemistry and hormones alone. She'd laid her heart bare in those short, tumultuous, unforgettable hours in bed. She'd loved him as no woman had ever loved him, wrenched emotions from him that he hadn't known existed, wrung him inside out with the force of her passion—and the power of her honesty.

The wimp had stolen his heart.

And Pax was starting to feel damn terrified that he'd never get it back.

He jammed the zinc sunscreen back into his pocket. "Good thing you don't live in the desert all the time, huh, Red?"

"I violently, vociferously hate it," she agreed amiably.

Pax kept telling himself that her enthusiastic revulsion for the desert—for his whole world—was one of the serious reasons why a future between them couldn't work. His father's desertion had irrevocably taught him that you couldn't force someone else to be happy, couldn't talk someone else into accepting or loving what you did. Such things were matters of the heart—and no one could have a more vulnerable or impulsive heart than Kansas.

A dozen times over the past few days, her words had come back to haunt him. No one can love you, she'd said. Unless you let them. Kansas saw love as a choice.

Pax saw a choice, too. The power to make a choice not to hurt her, not to be swayed by anything as uncertain as love, not to buy into a pipe dream about a future that had little prayer of working in reality.

"You need a drink," he told her, and uncapped his canteen.

She shook her head. "Not thirsty. Not right now."

"Yeah, well, you use up a ton of water when you're hiking, sweet pea. And you don't mess around with dehydration. A couple of sips. Come on."

"I am only obeying you, Mr. Bossy," she informed him, and took a quick slug from the canteen, "because I feel so guilty." She motioned to his pack...and hers. His weighed in around sixty pounds. He was carrying food for two, water for two, a sleeping bag, a range of first-aid supplies, emergency and cooking gear. She was carrying a sleeping bag and some personal items. "This isn't fair," she said—for about the tenth time.

"Fair isn't always equal. I built up stamina from doing this for years. No reason for you to feel guilty." He'd pared down her pack to less than fifteen pounds, and still she looked bedraggled and dead beat. No way she could have handled more. "Your leg holding up okay?"

"My leg's fine."

She met his eyes squarely, which made him suspicious. He'd seen Kansas meet his eyes before and hand out a bald-faced lie without a qualm of conscience. He hadn't caught her limping yet, and their slow pace would compensate for the rugged track if she'd just let it. Unfortunately Kansas—being Kansas—was so busy looking for snakes and gila monsters that she wasn't really inclined to notice where she was walking.

"If the leg acts up, we stop. Period."

"Hey. Just because I'm a wimp and a wuss, Doc, don't start thinking I'm prissy. I'm doing fine. And you warned me this would be my worst nightmare, didn't you?" Muttering and groaning, she pulled on the straps of her backpack again. "Let's get this show on the road and get it over with."

The worst nightmare for her wasn't the hiking trek, but the worrying about her brother. Pax knew every time Case crossed her mind. The dance and sparkle left her eyes, and like now, she plowed ahead with her jaw locked in a determined line. He strongly suspected that an avalanche had better not try to get between her and Case at this point. He also suspected she'd keep going if both her legs were broken.

When Kansas loved—she *loved*—with no glance at the cost or risk to herself. Pax knew that intimately well after making love with her, but that memory replaying in his mind was both a wonder and a curse. Her giving nature was unforgettable...but it also aroused his sense of honor. Kansas had no instinct at all for protecting herself. Either he took care of her, or it wasn't going to happen.

She started limping ten minutes before they reached the campsite, but he had her settled and off her feet in short order. Dinner was simple—Apache fried bread, dried meat, fruit. The site he'd chosen was the natural shelter of a limestone ledge; the ground beneath was harder than stone but flat enough to set up sleeping bags.

Pax had already explained to Kansas why he'd made certain choices about routing and timing. Because the kids needed to carry in supplies, they had probably chosen the northern route into Valle de Oro, which was easier and smoother and could have accommodated horses. He'd chosen the tougher, hiking route because it cut down more than a day of traveling. No matter what shape her brother was in, they could get in and out faster, and he'd planned an overnight because a sleepover gave them an advantage in timing. Neither knew what they were getting into with this group. If the kids were messing with hallucinogens and drugs, it made the most logistical sense to hit the camp at daybreak, when everyone would likely be sleeping.

Kansas hadn't argued with any of his plan—beyond giving him credit for having the miraculous brilliance to find the place.

There'd been no miracle or brilliance involved. Back in Nogales, Miguel only had to mention a few details about this *Valle de Oro* to stir Pax's memory bank. As a young man, he had hiked these mountains endlessly. Although the name was unfamiliar, he clearly recalled coming across a "golden valley"—a mesa bathed in gold, a magical, mystical trick of the morning sunlight. The silence and beauty of the place was unforgettable. He'd guessed then that it had to be a holy spot for the ancients, and especially in those years, he'd felt a strong simpatico with those who'd sought a private haven for meditation.

When his father left him, he'd had a lot of emotions to work through. For a long time, he'd wondered what the hell kind of worthless, unlovable son he'd been to make his father desert him. He'd dwelled on what he might have done, should have done, to reach his father, who'd been restless and melancholic ever since his mother died.

He really hadn't been conscious of verbally sharing those old memories until Kansas piped up.

"You don't have any idea if he's dead or alive, Pax?"

"No." They'd finished eating and cleaning up and set out the sleeping bags side by side. The sun was dropping fast now, the temperature plummeting with it. He dropped a sweatshirt over her shoulders, then stretched out next to her. "In the last years before he left, he drank his share, couldn't hold a job. But that wasn't the dad I grew up with. He completely changed after my mother died. He just wasn't the same man. It was like she was the thread that held him together. He lost all his laughter, all meaning in life."

"Horse feathers," Kansas said sharply.

He turned his head, startled by the sudden vehemence in her tone. It was late now. The sky had turned a deep, royal purple, the ledge overhang so shadowed that he could barely see her face.

"He had *you.* He had the responsibility of a son— you'd just lost your mom, too. He wasn't the only one going through grief—and he always had you to love. There was huge meaning in his life. He just dropped the ball. And personally, I think he should have been strung up by a rope for being such a selfish jerk as to leave you like that."

Normally the instinct would have been automatic to defend his father, yet Pax found his throat suddenly dry. He'd seen evidence of her unconditional loyalty before, but he'd never expected it to be showered on him. "I coped fine."

"That's not the point. If you were seventeen, weren't you in the middle of a school year?"

"Yeah. Finished out without letting anyone know."

"You never told anyone that you were alone?" The shock in her eyes shone even in the gathering darkness.

''Well, at first, I kept thinking he'd come back. And when he didn't...well, I just didn't know what would happen if I told. I was afraid of being uprooted, forced to go into a stranger's home or have some stranger have authority over my life. I knew how to cook. I got a job, after school and weekends, working for the local vet. I made enough to pay the bills.''

''So that's how you came to be a vet? Because of working with one?''

''Yeah. Old Henry Willis. Gruff, bad tempered—couldn't stand people—but he had hands with an animal like I couldn't believe. He pushed me into applying for vet school. My grades were good enough to get me in and cop a small academic scholarship—I worked the rest of the way. Every year, though, I got a cashier's check for a couple thousand bucks. I know damn well it was from Henry, although I never could get him to admit it.''

''You're talking about him in the past tense. He died?''

''Yes. When I was in school. No one told me. I didn't know until I came home from college that summer—'' Abruptly Pax fell silent, suddenly aware how long he'd been talking about himself. Damned if he understood how Kansas kept doing this to him. He never talked about personal history, ever. Except with her. "Before it gets pitch-black, we'd better get settled down for the night," he said briskly.

"You're right." Kansas peered out, as if she were just now noticing the landscape around them. From their tuck of an overhang, jagged hills stretched for miles, blanketed with windswept gnarled cotton trees and dusty cactus. A pale moon was rising. To Pax, the crisp air and stillness and silver-blue glow on the hills was the stuff of beauty and peace. For a moment, he thought—hoped—that Kansas might see the same beauty that he did.

"I guess I thought a desert was automatically like the Sahara," she mused. "All bleak sand and barrenness, nothing alive, nothing growing. I never expected to see the trees, the endless variety of plants."

It was the first positive thing she'd said about his country. Pax had the strangest inclination to hold his breath...but as he might have anticipated, her appreciation was short-lived.

"Probably an endless variety of critters thriving out there, too," she muttered darkly. Hunching down, she swiftly gathered up, face cream, toothbrush, canteen and a hairbrush. "I'm off to find a place to do my nightly ablutions. I won't be long. This definitely isn't the place for a sybaritic jasmine scented bath and a manicure.''

''Don't go far.''

''Don't go far, the man says. If I weren't suffering from a little modesty, I wouldn't even consider going out of your sight. And I'm warning you now, Doc, if I see even the teensiest snake—''

''I can't imagine that I would have any problem locating you, Red. I've heard your scream before.''

''Good,'' she said. ''Then you're prepared.''

When she disappeared from sight, Pax stared after her, thinking: no. From the day he'd met her, he'd never been prepared for Kansas.

But her mind was on her brother, and one way or another, her sole reason to be in this part of the country would be resolved tomorrow. He could surely keep her safe for such a short time. Safe from the snakes and all the imaginary desert monsters she loved dreaming up.

And safe from him.

Ten

"Do snakes sleep?"

"How amazing. I could have sworn we'd already had this conversation—several times. There is nothing to worry about, Ms. Wuss. Desert nights get chipper, like this one. And once the temperature drops, a snake curls up and snuggles just like a bug in a rug. He has no interest in bothering you whatsoever."

"Hmm." He was right about the night turning chipper. Kansas had the down sleeping bag zipped to her neck. Stars salted the navy sky. The air was so crisp and clear that she could see the faces on the moon…but it was Pax's face that captured her attention. He was stretched out next to her in an identical sleeping bag, lying flat on his back with his eyes closed. ''Exactly what kind of snakes live in the desert?''

''You do *not* want to know that answer, Red.''

''Yeah, I do.''

Without opening his eyes, Pax sighed. A loud, distinctly masculine sigh. ''Western diamond-backs and sidewinders both live around here.'' He added swiftly, ''Sidewinders are fascinating. They're little squirts, and they got their name from their funny method of locomotion. They can't get any traction to move in loose sand, so they kind of throw their body in a sideways loop and propel themselves forward that way.''

''You're right. That's absolutely fascinating. How gruesomely do you die if they bite you?''

Another sigh. This one husky with patience. ''Should you get bitten—which you won't—I have a snakebite kit in my pack and I know what to do. You're not going to die. Gruesomely or otherwise. That's a promise. And I think it'd be a real, real good idea if you got your mind off snakes for a while.''

''Okay. We can talk about centipedes and scorpions and spiders and tarantulas and gila monsters—''

"Just for the record—are you planning on doing this all night? Worrying yourself to death?"

"It sure looks that way. I've got one thumbnail chewed down to the nub and my pulse is racing like a 747. Pax?"

"What?"

"I'm petrified. Every time I close my eyes, I imagine a snake slithering toward me, or a tarantula jumping on my face. Do you know what I think would be a good idea?"

"That is *not* a good idea, Red."

She propped up on an elbow. It struck her as fascinating that he'd filled in the blanks without her needing to voice the thought. He knew her that well now. And although he'd half slept through the first part of the conversation, she noticed that his eyes were suddenly wide open. "I think it's a *great* idea. We could just zip the sleeping bags together. And then you could protect me from all the snakes and tarantulas…oh." She snapped her fingers in the darkness. "I know what you're thinking. Let that ditsy redhead get close, and who knows if she'll jump your bones again. But if you'll notice, I've behaved myself for days. You were always right, you know."

Not too surprisingly, his tone was guarded. "Right about what, precisely?"

"You were right that once I find my brother,

I have to leave. I have a job, a family, a place I'm paying rent on back home. I'm not too proud to admit that you stir my soup, Doc, but I can't just leave a whole life hanging. It's not like we fit into each other's life-styles in any way. There couldn't be two people born who were less meant for each other—''

''Is there a prayer, Kansas, the smallest prayer that you might go to sleep and quit talking soon?''

''Not,'' she said, ''in my own sleeping bag. If I promise—if I swear to control my wayward impulses and not jump your bones—could I come over there with you?'' When he didn't immediately respond, she said, ''This is about tarantulas, Pax. Not sex. This is about nightmares. This is about a small, frail, pitifully wimpy woman who needs a big strong guy to protect her—''

''You could only sell me that horseradish the first day I met you, shortie. You're about as pitiful as an armed lion, and you wouldn't sing 'rescue me' if you were up to your neck in quicksand.''

''Heavens. Have we made headway. I didn't realize how well you'd come to know me,'' she murmured. ''Still, I think everyone needs rescuing sometimes. Especially from the screaming meemies in the night.''

Utter silence. Then a muttered, "Aw, hell." Then the slow, reluctant sound of zipper teeth sliding down. He yanked her sleeping bag closer—with her in it. A flashlight snapped on, ribboning a trail of light down the zippers of both sleeping bags until Pax found where to join them together. He got the zipper ladder started, then switched off the light and finished the connecting job in the darkness.

"You happy now?"

"Yes, Pax."

"No way to avoid close quarters, but don't start getting nervous. And dammit, there is nothing that's going to get to you in the night. Now believe it and go to sleep."

"Yes, Pax."

She lay as still as an angel for at least three minutes. Maybe five. Possibly he realized that she'd sold him a con job, but knowing Pax's strong protective streak, she guessed he'd be incapable of turning her down. Volunteering to be her protector against Things That Went Bump In The Night, though, never meant that he was volunteering for any other type of closeness. He turned on his side and laid unbudgably still. Every muscle in his body was poker stiff. If he had to quit breathing to avoid accidentally touching her, he was clearly willing to make the sacrifice.

Kansas sighed, the most innocent of sleepy sighs she could muster...and catapulted toward him.

The tension in that cave-dark overhang was suddenly volatile enough to spark lightning. The threat of spontaneous combustion certainly wasn't emanating from her. She was as limp as a dishrag.

With another slumberous sigh, she burrowed her cheek in the curve of his shoulder. She nudged a knee between his legs in the most innocent of moves to nest more comfortably. One arm easily, naturally, draped around his ribs...which accidentally left no place for *his* arm to go. Except on her.

He couldn't hold that arm in midair forever—not in the cramped confines of the sleeping bag. Eventually his big callused hand fell, heavy and warm, on her shoulder. His palm connected with fabric, seemed to hesitate, and then slid down her back to feel more of the fabric. He suddenly clutched it. Tight.

"What the hell are you wearing, Red?" His voice was a whisper, husky and raw. "You brought a satin nightgown? To sleep in the desert?"

"I wasn't about to buy all new clothes for one overnight camp out. This is what I had around. What can I say? Hopeless sissies wear hopeless sissy stuff."

"Kansas?"

"Hmm."

"You lied to me. You didn't climb into this sleeping bag because you were sissy-scared of tarantulas."

"True. I don't care a hoot about tarantulas, Doc. I care about you," she whispered, and lifted her face to catch the rough, hard, frustrated kiss that was already aiming for her. She doubted he heard her; momentarily Pax seemed more than a little consumed by a case of masculine aggravation. She rewarded him for venting it on her by nestling closer, kneading a sensual train of caresses down his back, and kissing him back. Thoroughly and completely.

He didn't want this, she knew. He didn't want to let go. Not with her. Not again.

And making him so miserable was nothing she'd planned. It had been a horrible physical day for a couch potato; she was whipped-tired, and she'd never stashed birth control in her gear because there was no chance of anything happening. Pax had made painfully clear that he didn't want to touch her again. It still hurt. Like a raw sore. And Kansas knew too well it took two to love. She couldn't force a man to care who was brick wall determined to keep a distance.

"Damn you, Kansas." His voice was lower than a whisper, harsher than a rasp, as he swept her beneath him. A spanking hard kiss suddenly involved tongues, suddenly turned wet and warm. Tenderness seeped into the taste of that kiss, although she knew Pax was still angry. Nothing upset him more than feeling helpless.

The irony struck her. What he feared most was exactly what she wanted for him. If it was within her power—a mighty precarious *if*—Pax would suffer unbearable helplessness before this was over. Her fingers trailed the scrape of whiskers on his jaw and trailed to the long, strong cords of his neck, where a naked pulse was beating like drums.

He *did* like that nightgown of hers. He rubbed the satin against her skin, kneading, clutching, his touch urgent and possessive. His chest was bare, but below he wore jockey shorts, and beneath that cotton she felt him, warm and hard against her thigh, throbbing with an urgent pulse beat of its own. She nipped his shoulder. She rubbed her breasts against his chest. She gave her sweetest, her deepest, her most desperate kisses, until he clawed in a lungful of air and swore at her again.

It was his fault. She didn't volunteer for heartache a second time, not for anyone. And Pax, damn him, already had an aching heart-hold on her soul.

But he should never have told her about his father. Kansas always understood his fear of dependence, because she'd suffered being dependent on others herself. She understood his need to be strong, because she equally valued strength herself. But she hadn't known that his father had fallen apart after his wife's death. She hadn't guessed that Pax could be afraid that needing someone too much could destroy a man.

It wouldn't do—leaving him believing that. Someone had to love Pax. Fiercely and well and thoroughly. Someone had to teach that man that you didn't get slammed in the teeth if you dared need someone else. Someone had to show him that loving someone was not automatically a source of hurt. Someone had to spoil him with love, given freely, because otherwise the damn man could well go through the rest of his life lonely.

And this was it. The only chance she had. Once she found her brother tomorrow, her sole excuse for being in Arizona disappeared. So she had a choice—to shut up and leave him alone. Or to share her heart with him. One last time.

Desire sizzled. Needs steamed. The confining space of the double sleeping bag wasn't working at all. A zipper skated down its track, freeing chilled midnight air to feather and cool their skin, but it didn't seem to help. He was burning up. So was she. He pushed up the satin nightgown; she pushed and battled with his jockey shorts. He groaned when she found him, as if he were a man in pain.

"You brought—?"

"No. It's a safe time."

"There is no safe time." There was sanity in his eyes for that leak of a second. But even in the darkness, she could see that his eyes were as black and luminous as Apache's tears, vulnerable with desire, fierce with needing her.

"This is right," she insisted, as aware of his sense of honor as her own. But this was not the same as being careless or irresponsible. A child from him could never be more wanted or loved. She had never been more sure of anything, a terrifying measure of how deeply she'd come to love him, but for right now, she was incapable of a discussion on biology. "I love you," she said, because her feelings were all she knew how to express.

His mouth came back to hers, tasting, taking, blocking out those words. When he was forced to inhale another surge of oxygen, though, she said again, "I love you. And you're just gonna have to suffer through being loved, Doc, because tonight, this one night, I swear I'm not going to give you any other choice."

An arrogant plan, she recognized. Particularly considering that somewhere en route she'd stopped being in charge of anything. Her limbs felt liquid and her mind spun wild on the rush of emotions invoked by his hands, his mouth, the electricity mercilessly generated by Pax which shot sparks through every intimate part of her body. He reared up to claim her, wrapping her legs tight around him, her warrior out of control and no longer even trying to be.

It was what she wanted for him. The right to let go, to discover that with someone you trusted, that feeling of perilous, terrifying vulnerability was a wondrous thing. The only nasty thing was...that wondrous sword was always two-edged. The first time they'd made love, he'd laid her heart as open as an exposed and fragile rose.

This time was worse. This time she knew all she was risking. Yet diving off a cliff with him was a celebration of what two people could bring each other. Pax was a disastrously fast learner.

She thought she was strong. She thought she knew everything about herself as a woman. Yet Pax opened doors to freedom—and vulnerability—in herself that she'd never guessed.

Afterward, she lay exhausted and exhilarated, waiting, waiting for her heartbeat to climb down from that heady stratosphere.

Pax was breathing even harder than she was. When he collapsed, he stretched on his side facing her. She could feel his eyes on her face. At first, she thought he was stunned-tired, not stunned in any emotional sense. Yet even moments later, even minutes later, even in that heavy-sweet pitch-black darkness, she could feel his dark, silent gaze...

"It's okay," she whispered. "You're still free, Pax. You were always free. Nothing's changed."

...drinking her in, inhaling her, memorizing her with such intensity that he seemed unwilling to even blink.

"Close your eyes, Doc."

Finally he did.

At daybreak, color stole over the sky in a pastel palette. There was no wonder the Spanish had named this place *Valle de Oro,* valley of gold. Light reflecting off the striated rock bathed even the spiny buckhorn chollas in a hazy halo of gold. The temperature was balmy; the whole world seemed softened and serene—except for his pain-punched heart.

Pax wasn't about to forget last night. He had never been a gambler, never anticipated having the feeling of gold dust sifting through his fingers. He hadn't realized what he had...until he faced losing it.

Kansas strode ahead of him, moving silent and fast. There was no reason for him to play leader and trail blazer, when their route was clear. Past the valley between the two breasts of hills was the mesa plain where the kids had set up their campsite.

She was wearing khaki slacks this morning, hik-ing boots and a photographer's pocket vest. Very L.L. Bean. Nothing like the vanilla-colored satin nightgown she'd worn the night before that had tipped the edge on his sanity. Even dressed in such totally out of character practical attire, though, her flame of hair, the swish in her behind, was noticeably and unforgettably Kansas.

She crouched down suddenly, to examine a plant on the cactus strewn path. He hustled to catch up with her, feeling an instinctive and familiar alarm—she had a long-standing, impulsive habit of touching things she shouldn't. And then he saw what she was studying.

She raised blinding-soft eyes to him. "This is datura, isn't it? The way it grows in the wild?"

"Yeah." The weed was easily identifiable, with big veiny leaves leading from thick stems, coarse in look and texture. "If you want to get technical, there's a difference between common datura—also known as jimsonweed, or stink-weed—and sacred datura. What you're looking at is sacred datura. It's a perennial, where its rag-tail relatives are all annuals."

"I read about that. I also read that our native people weren't the only ones to use it for visions. It was used during World War II as a truth serum in prison camps." She touched a leaf. "It's really this easy to find, is it? A poison like this just grows everywhere?"

He nodded. "It's a pretty common weed through the Southwest."

"It's ugly, Pax."

Yeah, it was, yet her judgment of the plant was obviously affected by her feelings about her brother. There was no surprise that she'd come to associate the desert with ugly, frightening things. She'd never had a chance to see the beauty.

She lurched to her feet, dusting her hands on

her fanny. The gesture was familiar, yet the expression on her face wasn't. For the first time since he met her, Kansas looked calm and cool and so damn quiet that she was scaring him.

"Red...if you're worried about what shape your brother is in, or what we might be walking into—"

"I'm not."

She had to be. Kansas was Kansas. She'd never hidden a single emotion before. Every feeling was always out there, reflected in her face as clear as a mirror. He said carefully, "I didn't want to upset you by talking about worst-case scenarios, but I've done rescues involving all kinds of medical emergencies before. I have a full pack of medical supplies, and I know how to use them. And if this group appears dangerous, we would make the obvious safe choice and split, hightail it back for some help from the law. I know you can't really be feeling this calm. If you're unsure about anything we're going to do—"

She shook her head with a faint smile. "I know we're facing all those unknowns. This could either go real tough or real easy, and we can't know that ahead of time. But I'm fine. In fact, I couldn't be feeling more calm or sure. There's just a level where none of those unknowns make any difference, because my role in this is the same no matter what. I love my brother. Whatever strength or help he needs from me, I intend to be there for him. Really, I'm okay with this.''

Sometimes, Pax mused, she showed such insight that she blew him away. It wasn't the first time he'd glimpsed the strength of cement beneath the whimsical, ethereal exterior. Yet he had a sudden, brief leaden feeling. Kansas wasn't exactly pushing him away, but an invisible distance was there. She wasn't asking for his help, not on this. She didn't need him.

He banished that sinking feeling—this was no time to deal with it. One turn past the sheltering shade of the hills, and there was the flat-plained mesa.

Kansas sucked in her breath when she saw the scene. A hundred yards away, smoke drifted from the night's ashes of a fire. A dozen pup tents and old army tents were arranged like a mini city around a central circle of stones. A few scruffy horses were tied on a lead line in the distance. The place was as quiet as a cemetery. There wasn't a sign of life stirring this early.

They dropped their packs and left them. Pax strode ahead, aiming for the largest tent, catching details from his peripheral vision. There were clothes strewn around. Shoes. Canned food spilling from boxes and packs. Near the fire pit, a slab of limestone was set up like an altar with burned-down candles laying in cold pools of wax. His jaw instinctively tightened.

If the biggest tent housed the head honcho, the boy certainly wasn't much. When Pax opened the flap, yellow desert sun shined like a shock into the eyes of a scrawny, unkempt kid who appeared to be naked. "What the—who are you?"

"I'm Dr. Moore and I'm looking for Case Walker. Which tent is he in?"

"What you want with him, man?"

"Just to talk with him. His sister is with me. And we can go from tent to tent and find him ourselves, but there doesn't seem any point in waking everyone up. He's the only one we're looking for."

The kid peered out far enough to glance at Kansas, then back at Pax. "Hey, we ain't doing nothing, man. Nothing that's anybody's business. We're not bothering anybody out here."

"I didn't say you were. Your private business is nothing to me. All I want is to talk with Case."

The boy seemed to think about that, then shrugged and motioned to one of the tents in the middle of the camp. "Far as I know, he sacked out in there last night."

It was that easy. There were no problems, no trouble—no one even stirred once the head honcho reclosed the flap on his tent with a yawn and settled down again. And Case was there. Exactly where the boy told them.

Only nothing, from that minute on, was easy for Kansas. Red headed for the sun-worn, faded pup tent at about the speed of light. When she knelt down and pushed at the screen flap, Pax knew she'd identified her brother, because her face drained of color.

"Kansas? It's really you? How can you be here...how'd you find me...what...?"

The last time Pax saw the boy, Case had a been a brawny-shouldered, hefty 200 pounds, with a mischievous devil in his eyes and the grin of a lady charmer. Maybe his hair had been combed last week. He'd easily lost twenty pounds. His eyes were dull, his cheeks hollow, and his whole expression looked disoriented and confused.

"Kansas," he said again, and though she answered him—and kept answering him—Case couldn't seem to stop repeating her name.

Kansas's voice turned as soothing and soft as butter, nothing to indicate she was distressed in any way. "When's the last time you had something to eat, Tiger?"

"I dunno."

"Well, we're gonna take care of that. I want you to come with me, okay? We'll leave your stuff, worry about all that later. Can you stand up?"

Case crawled out of the tent, but he stood up like a seaman who hadn't seen land in months, unsteady on his feet. The bright sunlight made him cringe, but he kept looking at her, saying "Kansas," as if her name was an anchor and he had no other.

"Yeah, Tiger. It's me. And I've brought a good friend to help us. Everything's going to be okay. All you have to do is lean on me." To Pax, she mouthed the word "hospital." He nodded.

It was a long trek back to the Explorer. Pax had been more frustrated. He just couldn't remember when. He'd done rescue missions before, had been prepared to carry or handle Case, no matter what was required or what condition the boy was in. He also had years of experience soothing wild animals and calming frightened people, but Case—there was no way that boy was turning to anyone but his sister.

Kansas talked nonsense to him the whole hike

out, her arm around Case's waist, supporting a grown man who was damn near twice her size. One minute Case was solid, the next he was hallucinating and imagining devils in every cactus, every cloud. He had an insatiable thirst. They stopped a dozen times, trying to pour water down him and coax in a little food.

Pax had seen Kansas claim an imminent heart attack over a tarantula, heard her screech bloody murder at the mere look of a gila monster. Yet when she had an outstandingly fine reason to really fall apart, her touch stayed calm, her voice stayed cool and no trace of stress even crossed her expression.

Once, he'd believed she was the most vulnerable woman he'd ever met.

He still believed that.

It had just taken him forever to understand that Kansas was also strong. His whole life, Pax had valued strength as a means of protecting himself—and others. But his Red had a core of emotional strength different than he'd ever defined the quality before. He wanted to think about that, wanted to examine how somehow she'd squeejawed and changed his whole understanding of what real strength was.

But there was no time, right then, to do anything but tackle the problem at hand. Handling

Case was a full-time job, mentally and physically, even after they'd finally gotten him home and into the clinic in Sierra Vista. Even after Dr. Lowrey finished his examination and met up with them in the waiting room.

"Long term, he should have no trouble regaining his physical health. There's no sign of any permanent damage to his organs, which was obviously our first worry. And some of his physical problems will improve in a matter of days. He's suffering more from exhaustion and dehydration than anything else."

"What about mentally?" Kansas asked quietly.

The doctor had gentle ways and old, tired eyes. "Mentally he's confused. Your brother doesn't seem to be aware that he's been under the influence of a drug. He says he's never touched anything but some natural herbs." Dr. Lowrey sighed. "This is the second case I've handled this year involving datura. Unlike peyote, I don't think you need to fear an addiction in the same sense as a narcotic. But any use of this type of hallucinogen can have emotional as well as physical effects. Damage to his heart was the first fear, but his heart is fine. He needs rest, food, care...and time. He's essentially been taking a poison, whether he understood that or not."

They only talked for a few more minutes after the doctor left, and then Kansas walked down the hall with him. Once she called her parents and filled them in, she planned to stay overnight in the room with Case. For as long as her brother was confused, she wasn't about to leave him. Pax understood why she wanted to stay, but he felt a sudden emptiness. He didn't want to leave her alone in that stark, antiseptic hall. He didn't want to leave her at all.

But they'd put plans in motion for him, too. "All right. I'm on my way to track down the sheriff," he told her.

"Good. I can hardly stand to think of the rest of those kids being in that camp even one more night. You make sure he listens, Pax."

"I will...and I'll bring you some stuff tomorrow."

"Thanks." She grinned. "By tomorrow morning I'll be awfully desperate for a toothbrush." She raised up and kissed him on the cheek. "Thanks, you. For everything. You never once had to help me, Doc, but from the very beginning you came through like a white knight."

She was only saying good-night, not dismissing him. It had been an unbearably long and exhausting day, and she was weaving on her feet. There was no reason for him to stay; she didn't need him and he had things to do—the sheriff to see, animals to feed and care for. But it felt like goodbye, that kiss. It felt like a gut-sharp reminder that Kansas had no reason, once Case recovered enough to be discharged from the clinic, to stay in Arizona.

To stay with him.

Eleven

Kansas lingered at the airport until the plane disappeared from sight. Well, it was done. Her brother was winging home, and their parents were set up to meet his flight in Minneapolis. Case was a long way from running marathons, but her mom, typically, had turned rock solid the minute she had the complete story on Case's health condition. Her brother couldn't be in better hands.

Kansas headed for her rental car, feeling as fidgety and restless as a Mexican jumping bean. Case was being taken care of. She wasn't so sure about herself.

She drove straight to a grocery store with the goal of picking up empty boxes. It was too soon to buy her own plane ticket home to Minnesota. Case's belongings needed to be packed and sent home, his bills taken care of and his bank account closed, then something done with the landlord about his rental place.

If she worked like a dog, she figured the chores could probably get done in a day. If she stretched them out, it could possibly take three. There was no way she could make them last a decade, yet the minute she thought about leaving, her pulse started thumping like an agitated battery gone berserk.

She'd already told herself the obvious: you couldn't lose a man that you'd never won. Inventing excuses to stay were never going to change the bottom line. She'd offered Pax her heart every which way she knew how. Either her brand of love wasn't enough, or Pax simply didn't want it.

Yet an hour later, when she zoomed in the driveway with a back seat and trunkful of empty packing boxes, Pax was there. Waiting for her. Instead of his Explorer, he'd driven a battered old Jeep that she hadn't seen before. He was leaning against the side, his hands slugged into his pockets, his lean face taking a battering from the midday desert sun.

He sprang forward to help her carry the packing boxes into the house. "I just stopped by to tell you what happened. The sheriff organized a whole crew—parents, medics, local ranchers, the forest rangers. The kids have been cleared out of there."

"Thank heavens." As soon as Pax pushed open the door, she dropped an armload of boxes onto the living room floor. "I don't know if any of those kids realized what they were getting into. Case wasn't looking for drugs. Or trouble. He was looking for meaning. And I couldn't stop thinking that was possibly how some of these religious cults start—from some real innocent and idealistic motivations, simply misinterpreted and taken too far." She shook her head. "I'm relieved that the sheriff intervened before it went any farther. And no one would have taken action if you hadn't become involved, Doc."

"Yeah, well…the whole community should have paid attention to what was happening long before this."

It was so typical of Pax to take responsibility but no credit, but just then she didn't want to argue with him. She wanted to savor the look of him. No different than always, he was a sun-browned, strong warrior, a mountain of an unforgettable man...yet for the first time since she'd known him, he was nervously, uneasily shifting on his feet.

"I can see you have packing and things to do for your brother yet. I should have called before stopping by."

"That's okay."

"I don't suppose you could spare a little time? Like a few hours?"

"Sure." She lifted her eyebrows.

Pax abruptly locked in his heels and looked stubborn. "Now, I know you think of the desert as a nightmare. I know you think you hate it. But, Red...you've been worried about your brother the whole time you were here. And before you go back home, well, I'd just like to show you *my* desert. So you don't leave thinking there's nothing to love in this part of the country."

Oh Pax, she thought fiercely. *I already found more to love here than I can possibly handle.* But she just said, "I can go right now, if you want."

Miles back, Pax turned off the blacktop and aimed down the two-track gravel road. Although his Explorer was tough, it couldn't compete with his old, open Jeep in true rough country, and he knew exactly where he wanted to take her. She'd seen datura and gila monsters. She'd seen the ugly, bleak, frightening side of the desert—but she'd never seen the beauty.

Just as the hummingbird migration in Ramsey Canyon only lasted a short time, his desert was only in bloom for the blink of an eye. That time was now or never—but a man had to know exactly what he was looking for. The Arizona Rainbow was only one of the cacti blossoming right now, with big, deep pink flowers. Other plants, like the Queen of the Night, looked like dead scrub during the day, yet its bloom was a huge eight inches in breadth with an exquisite fragrance at nighttime. The Santa Rita prickly pear had delicate lemon yellow flowers.

The desert blossoms were all fragile, all fleeting, all impossibly vulnerable—like Kansas, he thought. A vice gripped his heart at the idea of her leaving. He had the despairing feeling it would be like losing all his sunshine. She'd opened doors in his life that had been locked for years. He hadn't once shared back—not the way she did. Somehow he had to show her how much she'd changed his life, and he had no idea how to do that, except by taking her somewhere that deeply, privately mattered to him.

Abruptly he picked up a strange, hot metallic

smell. Within seconds, he caught a plume of smoke coming from under the Jeep's hood. He quickly scanned the gauges.

"What's wrong?" Kansas asked.

There should be nothing wrong. In this part of the country, a man took care of his vehicles the way a cowboy took care of his horse. Neither his Explorer nor his Jeep had ever been neglected—yet the temperature gauge suddenly glared red. Pax cut the engine and coasted to a stop with his forehead creased in an exasperated scowl. "Don't worry."

"I'm not worried."

"Doesn't matter what it is. I'll handle it. There's nothing you need to worry about."

"I couldn't be less worried," she repeated amiably.

Well, he sure was. His gaze swept the landscape—there was nothing around, no houses, no people, no cars anywhere in sight. Hell, that was why he'd wanted to take her here—the spot was a secluded, private haven, a secret he'd wanted to share only with her.

But he was rattled as he vaulted out of the Jeep. Protecting a woman was one of the maxims of his life. Getting her stranded in the midday heat of the desert had definitely *not* been on the day's agenda.

He flipped the catch on the hood. Kansas bounced out of the passenger side and slapped on a hat—a silly big-brimmed hat with giant yellow flowers. It was so whimsical and pure female—and just like her—that for a second, he had to grin.

Quickly, though, he yanked the rod in place to hold up the hood so he could peer in the engine. Heaven knew how it happened. Maybe he'd been looking at that hat. Or maybe his conscience was shooting panic darts at the idea of anything happening to her in his care. But somehow he must not have secured the rod well enough, because the hood came slamming down. He jerked back fast enough to save his head—but not his wrist. The hood smashed down at such a wrong angle that he saw stars.

Dammit, he wasn't a man to see stars. And he sure as hell wasn't a man prone to carelessness. Ever.

"My Lord!" Kansas rushed toward him.

"It's nothing. I'm fine."

"Horseradish, you're fine!" It only took seconds for his wrist to turn red and start swelling big time.

"I'll be all right in a minute," he said, yet he could feel all the nuisance symptoms of shock—

clammy hands, light-headedness. Nothing he had the patience or time to cope with.

"If it were me, I'd be crying my eyes out... subjecting you to a whole tantrum of moans and noisy, pitiful groans. Don't you want to vent a little?"

Kansas was cracking jokes, but of course she didn't realize how much trouble they were in. His mind cataloged the situation with reeling speed. The Jeep was good and dead. He guessed a stone must have caused the hole in the radiator, and naturally he carried emergency water, but even a full jerrycan couldn't overcome a leak that size. There was no way to call for help, because he'd never transferred the car phone from his Explorer. Hell, he'd never expected to need a phone for a few short hours, and he wanted this time alone with Kansas without the risk of interruptions.

There were no good options in sight. Pax didn't think his wrist was broken, but temporarily he couldn't move it for love or money. They couldn't hike. Not in this heat. Dehydration was too serious a risk with the distance they'd have to walk back to a civilized road.

In the cool of the night, they could hike out, but for now, their best choice was to rest in cool shade until the heat of the day passed. Since there was no shade, that meant they literally had to create some—which, as he explained to Kansas, meant digging a hole under the Jeep and lying directly in it.

"I don't think I can do it, Red," he said gruffly.

"Well, of course you can't, Doc. Good thing you brought me along, huh? And heavens, I haven't had such a terrific adventure in a blue moon!"

This was a catastrophe, not an adventure. She was never going to understand the joy or beauty he found in the desert, not when every experience she'd had was a pit load of stress.

Yet Kansas made out like she'd never been happier. She found the minisurvival shovel in the back of his Jeep and set to work like an intrepid female Indiana Jones. His city slicker should have balked at the idea of lying under the Jeep for hours—it wasn't precisely a romantic view, looking up at the stinky, cramped, dirty underside of a vehicle. Her white shorts were destroyed before it was done; she had sand on her hair, on her neck; she'd lost a nail, her hat and an earring.

Yet by four in the afternoon, she was still having a party. She had to be starving, but she never complained. She'd wrapped his wrist in a rag soaked in canteen water and told him every dirty joke she knew—her repertoire was extensive. She was moving into sick, sick limericks when they both suddenly heard the sound of a car engine.

"Well, darn. I hope the mounties haven't arrived. Right when we were having so much fun!" She scooched out, looked up, and then reported back. "It's not the mounties," she said gloomily, "but it sure looks like a potential rescue vehicle. I suppose I'd better get out there and flash some leg." She ducked her head and blessed him with a cheeky grin. "Although with these skinny legs, we're probably risking the guy speeding up instead of stopping."

The rancher didn't speed up. He stopped to help, used the cellular phone in his pickup to call a tow truck, and then insisted on driving them all the way back to Pax's place. Kansas pushed that plan because Ms. Bossy was determined that his wrist get medical attention ASAP. As soon as they arrived home, she took the wheel of the Explorer and aimed straight for the emergency room.

Pax was used to rescuing. Not *being* rescued. A long, tediously exasperating two hours later, the doctor had put him through X rays, stuffed him with painkillers and anti-inflammatants, and ace-bandaged his wrist. Kansas was still listening to the doctor's instructions when Pax had had it with all the mollycoddling and took off like a bat out of hell.

She drove him home, and just as if she owned the place, came right in. The cats swarmed all over both of them like locusts. Red fed them first, crooning baby talk to even the mangiest, then foraged in the fridge for a makeshift dinner for the two of them, cleaned that up faster than a dizzy whirlwind and then—out of nowhere—stopped abruptly in the middle of the kitchen and looked him over head to toe.

''Pax,'' she said critically, ''you look like something one of your cats would be ashamed to drag home. I swear you could scare small children if you went out in public.''

''Ah, Red? You're lacking a little glamour yourself right now.''

''Exactly my point. A shower's in order. You want some more of those pain pills first?''

No, he didn't want any more pain pills. He wanted this Murphy's Law of a horrible day erased off the map. She'd never said one word about his being a klutzy screw-up. But it bit. Like wolf teeth. He'd *needed* this day, needed it to be right, for her, with her. He'd taken care of people his whole adult life with no sweat, when the only woman in the whole damn universe he wanted to take care of was her—and he'd flopped like a dead pansy.

Kansas had taken to ordering him around like a pint-size marine sergeant—a marine sergeant with the devil in her eyes. "Poor baby, we'd better cover that wrist with a plastic bag to keep it dry in the shower—and you'll probably need a little help stripping."

His wrist was annoyingly immobile and it hurt, but it was never an injury he was going to die from. No one ever pampered him in his entire life, for pete's sake, and he could peel off his own clothes. Still, there was no stopping her from fussing and flying around. She hustled up a plastic bag, ferreted out thick, fresh towels, nosed in his closet for clean clothes, then turned on the shower. Apparently she planned to supervise his stripping down, too, because she stood there with her hands on her hips and a bulldog-determined tilt in her chin.

So he kissed her. It was a wild impulse, that kiss, but a tornado couldn't have stopped it—or him. The impulse seemed to have been stored up all day, maybe as long as the last time they'd made love, maybe...all his life.

She quit moving like a dizzy-fast magpie. She

quit flying around like a flashy hummingbird. She just stood there then, quiet like she hadn't once been quiet all day, her face lifted to his, inhaling that tender, deep, dark, endless kiss until neither of them had a lick of air in their lungs.

"Pax..." Her voice had turned slow and soft, but the question in her eyes never got said.

"Hey, I'm not the only one who needs a shower," he teased her...and when he climbed in, pulled her in with him. The drenching spray muffled her startled gasp of laughter. She was still clothed. Temporarily. He fumbled one-handed to peel off her sodden duds under the warm deluge. It took a while. It took a while for all the desert sand to sluice down the drain, too, but by the time they were both squeaky clean, Kansas was no longer chortling with laughter. She was just looking at him, with a yearning invitation in those vulnerable china blue eyes.

He couldn't carry her, but he wrapped her warm and dry in one towel and lassoed her with a second one. Possibly he didn't need to rope her into following him into his bedroom—Kansas knew the way.

She shimmied out of that towel like a born stripper and came to him, still damp, her half-dried hair flying every which way, and leveled him on the king-size bed. "Now listen, slugger, you're not up for a wrestling match,'' she told him. ''Not with that wrist. So you're just going to have to suffer being spoiled.''

Kansas had that real, real wrong. She was the one who needed spoiling and treasuring, and a sprained wrist wasn't about to stop him. His whole life, he'd sought peace. She'd ruined any chance he could find it without her. Before Kansas, he'd buried his emotions like roots in hibernation. She'd dragged them all out and exposed them to the sun. She'd scared him with her foolhardy impulsiveness. She'd nosed into private corners of his life. Worst of all, she'd generously and openly accepted him—not for what he could do, not for his strength and the hundred things people counted on him for. But for just who he was.

She seemed to love him the most when he was at his worst, his weaknesses laid bare. Kansas just never understood that she was entirely different than any other woman in the universe—at least his universe—and it hurt like a sword slash that he'd failed to tell her what she meant to him.

He wanted her to know she was loved. He wanted her to *feel* loved, with everything that was in him. He showed her his heart with kisses and caresses, and by taking her, with languid-liquid cherishing slowness, the way he should have made love to her a long time ago.

"Oh, Pax," she whispered when it was over. "Oh, Pax." And then she murmured in the darkness, "I love you."

Wrapped in his arms, she fell into a doze before he'd returned the emotion in words. It didn't matter, he thought. It was something he hadn't understood before. No matter how insurmountable any problem appeared, nothing mattered more than being with her. Tomorrow, they would have time to talk, but this whole day had been an exhausting blinger for both of them. Snuggling her closer, he closed his eyes.

But in the morning, when he woke up, she was gone.

By sheer luck Kansas found a flight that still had empty seats. She bought her ticket, checked her bags and then headed for the airline waiting area. Most of the plastic chairs were empty—her flight wouldn't leave for more than an hour—but she couldn't sit. She made her way to the long glass windows, her gaze fixed on the bleak, hot, blue desert sky.

Her eyes were stinging dry and her stomach was knotted in a lump of loss. Climbing out of Pax's bed and leaving him was one of the hardest things she'd ever done. But at five in the morning, she'd been at her brother's place, boxing the last of his clothes, then packing her own. Case's other business chores would have to be handled long distance. She couldn't stay. Not even a day longer.

Kansas told herself that it was way past time she accepted that she had gambled her heart... and lost.

Yesterday kept replaying in her mind, because their Jeep breaking down in the desert seemed to underline the bridge they couldn't cross. Pax, she'd always known, perceived needing others as a weakness. When he injured his wrist, he'd been stuck needing her. She'd tried to joke and make him laugh, but she could see how badly it bothered him. Pax would never willingly depend on her. The right to be there was a privilege that came with love, but Kansas couldn't force him to see that.

"Flight 346 is now boarding through Gate Six," a woman's voice announced over the loudspeaker.

Her flight. Woodenly Kansas plucked at her purse straps and aimed for the back of the line, noting vaguely that the waiting area had filled up with passengers. Typically she didn't fit in. Most of the crowd were dressed in khaki and neutral colors, compared to her overbright green jumpsuit. Clothes had been the last thing on her mind that morning, but she wouldn't have worried about it anyway.

People had always seemed determined to judge her on surface appearances, never realizing that a shrimp-size set of bones or a showy exterior might not be the whole picture. She was strong. She just wasn't strong by the rules most people played by. Funny, but she'd really believed Pax saw that. She'd really believed he was the only one, ever in her life, to respect and value the kind of strong woman she was...and wanted to be.

Someone barreled through the doors behind her. She ignored all the jostling as she pawed through the debris in her purse, searching for the plane ticket that should have been in plain sight and wasn't. She glanced up. There. Over by the windows on the floor. She'd dropped it like a scatterbrained ditz.

Tears sprang to her eyes. Pretty darn crazy to cry over an almost-lost ticket, yet she blinked back the first round, and the bucket filled again. Well, spit. It appeared she was going to wimp out in public big time. Worse, she couldn't care less.

She headed blindly for the ticket, yet even

with her vision blurred and slurred, she never anticipated the sudden collision with a brick wall. Big strong hands clutched her shoulders, steadying her, and then squeezed around her so tightly she couldn't breathe or see. "Dammit, Kansas. You stole my Explorer, and with the Jeep dead, I had to track down a neighbor who could loan me a set of wheels. I didn't know where you were. When I didn't find you at your brother's, I thought you'd left. I thought I'd missed you."

She forgot the plane. She forgot the ticket on the floor. She struggled to believe the emotion she heard in his voice. "I didn't mean to steal your Explorer, but I didn't have any other way to get back to my rental car. And I thought it'd help. I thought it'd be easier for you...if I just made a clean break."

"Well, you had that real wrong, Red. Because I don't want a break from you. Ever." Pax gently eased his knuckles under her chin so he could see her face. And she saw his. Grave lines of strain were harshly etched on his brow. His whole face was stiff with anxiety. And his eyes were so black and vulnerable with such fierce love that she suddenly couldn't swallow. "I'm asking you to stay."

"Stay?"

"I know how you feel about the desert. But if you'll just give it some time—give me some time—I think we could change your mind about it. We could try. And if that doesn't work, we could give your big green woods in Minnesota a try." He sucked in a breath. "Hell, I don't care if we live on the North Pole. Please stop crying, Red."

"I was just crying because I thought I'd lost the plane ticket."

"No doubt." The pad of his thumb smoothed away a salty tear. "I'm guessing you're always going to cry for important things like that. Just like you're always gonna scream bloody murder for a spider. You really are a hopeless wimp, Red."

"I told you I was. I told you that from the very beginning."

"I know you did." His fingertips soothed away another tear. "And the first time I met you, I thought holy kamoly. Someone's got to protect that woman or she's going to get herself seriously hurt. Every time I turned around, you were diving off a cliff for your brother. You dove off a cliff for me, too. You're the most reckless woman I know, Kansas. And the strongest, even if it took me forever to figure that out. And I don't know how I could love you more."

A door opened somewhere. The scream of jet engines firing up was earsplitting loud for a second, and then the door closed. The plane was about to take off, she realized. And so was her heart.

"I never thought you'd say it." She looped her arms around his neck. She kissed his chin, to make him smile. And then surged up on tiptoe, to give him more kisses. Rich, warm, wildly impulsive kisses, until that horrible anxiety disappeared from his face and the tension eased out of his shoulders. "I never thought you'd see it."

"I saw it. I just didn't know how to tell you. Words come real rusty to a man who's been living in a barren desert." He smoothed back her hair, touching her, unable to stop touching her. "I think I loved you before I even met you. I think I was waiting for you in every lonely moment in my life. But you may have to be patient, Red. Believe me, I'll work on it, but it may take me fifty, sixty years of practice before I learn to be as open and loving as you are."

"Fifty years?" If her throat wasn't jammed with so much emotion, she might have been able to say something more coherent.

"I know. It's a long time. We should probably start with a ring and follow that up with a houseful of kids.'' He upped the ante fast. ''I swear I'll get rid of the cats.''

''I love the cats.''

''Okay, we'll keep the cats.''

''I like your desert just fine, too. I never thought it would happen, but somehow I've become fond of your Arizona heat. Um, Pax? I don't know if you noticed that plane just taking off, but I'm afraid it has all my clothes on it.''

He didn't look at the plane. He didn't even glance out the window. His eyes were on her face, and for a man who once fought to never show emotion, the depth and fierce tenderness in his expression was more than enough to make her heart tumble and soar. ''You won't need to worry about clothes for a long while, Kansas.''

The same thought crossed her mind. Eventually she'd need clothes. Eventually she'd have to trek north to settle her job and her apartment and introduce Pax to her family. But right now she had other priorities.

Pax had been a warrior for a long time, she thought. He was used to being strong. But he wasn't used to believing anyone would be there for him. He had finally figured out that the source of real strength was the courage to reach out and share your heart. The rest would come. If it took her a lifetime of spoiling that man, she was more than up for the job.

She reached up to kiss him...a kiss that started out soft and sweet and swiftly turned intimate and deeply private. The kind of kiss that belonged only to Pax, the kind he'd always inspired in her and with her. "I hope you weren't counting on a peaceful life, Doc, because I plan to give you a lot of trouble," she whispered.

"I hope that's a promise."

"You bet it is." She smiled for him. "Take me home, love."

* * * * *